HEART OF GOLD

SEAL Brotherhood: Legacy Series

Book 7

SHARON HAMILTON

SHARON HAMILTON'S BOOK LIST

SEAL BROTHERHOOD BOOKS

SEAL BROTHERHOOD SERIES

Accidental SEAL Book 1

Fallen SEAL Legacy Book 2

SEAL Under Covers Book 3

SEAL The Deal Book 4

Cruisin' For A SEAL Book 5

SEAL My Destiny Book 6

SEAL of My Heart Book 7

Fredo's Dream Book 8

SEAL My Love Book 9

SEAL Encounter Prequel to Book 1

SEAL Endeavor Prequel to Book 2

Ultimate SEAL Collection Vol. 1 Books 1-4 /2 Prequels

Ultimate SEAL Collection Vol. 2 Books 5-7

SEAL BROTHERHOOD LEGACY SERIES

Watery Grave Book 1

Honor The Fallen Book 2

Grave Injustice Book 3

Deal With The Devil Book 4

Paradise: In Search of Love
Love Me Tender, Love You Hard

NOVELLAS
SEAL You In My Dreams Magnolias and Moonshine

PARANORMALS

GOLDEN VAMPIRES OF TUSCANY SERIES
Honeymoon Bite Book 1
Mortal Bite Book 2
Christmas Bite Book 3
Midnight Bite Book 4

THE GUARDIANS
Heavenly Lover Book 1
Underworld Lover Book 2
Underworld Queen Book 3
Redemption Book 4

FALL FROM GRACE SERIES
Gideon: Heavenly Fall

SUNSET BEACH SERIES
I'll Always Love You

NOVELLAS
SEAL Of Time Trident Legacy

All of Sharon's books are available on Audible,
narrated by the talented J.D. Hart.

ABOUT THE BOOK

Tyler has been a Navy SEAL for nearly ten years and he's wearing out. The prospect of doing another re-up has him worried that his body, banged up, shot, stabbed and multiple bones broken, can't take any more. After performing over a thousand HALO jumps in hostile territory and five times that in practice jumps, he thinks perhaps he's run out of time and is concerned he'll suffer permanent disabilities if he pushes the envelope too far.

But, like a professional athlete, giving up the life he loves, working out and doing missions with his best buds from SEAL Team 3, something he knew he was made for, he can't see himself doing anything else. Certainly not anything as exciting.

He has choices, especially if he wants to keep his wife happy, even if he gives up some of the glory and glamor of being a member the elite warrior class. And he would like to be able to chase his three kids around in something other than a wheelchair.

But an enemy from the past has appeared in the shadows, forcing Tyler to make a decision that might ruin his marriage, and cost him his cherished family.

Which is more important, his promise or the safety of the ones he loves?

AUTHOR'S NOTE

I always dedicate my SEAL Brotherhood books to the brave men and women who defend our shores and keep us safe. Without their sacrifice and that of their families—because a warrior's fight always includes his or her family—I wouldn't have the freedom and opportunity to make a living writing these stories. They sometimes pay the ultimate price so we can debate, argue, go have coffee with friends, raise our children, and see them have children of their own.

One of my favorite tributes to warriors resides on many memorials, including one I saw honoring the fallen of WWII on an island in the Pacific:

> "When you go home
> Tell them of us, and say
> For your tomorrow,
> We gave our today."

These are my stories created out of my own imagination. Anything that is inaccurately portrayed is either my mistake or done intentionally to disguise something I might have overheard over a beer or in the corner of one of the hangouts along the Coronado Strand.

I support two main charities. Navy SEAL/UDT Museum operates in Ft. Pierce, Florida. Please learn about this wonderful museum, all run by active and former SEALs and their friends and families, and who rely on public support, not that of the U.S. Government. www.navysealmuseum.org

I also support Wounded Warriors, who tirelessly bring together the warrior as well as the family members who are just learning to deal with their soldier's condition and have nowhere to turn. It is a long path to becoming well, but I've seen first-hand what this organization does for its warriors and the families who love them. Please give what your heart tells you is right. If you cannot give, volunteer at one of the many service centers all over the United States. Get involved. Do something meaningful for someone who gave so much of themselves, to families who have paid the price for your freedom. You'll find a family there unlike any other on the planet. www.woundedwarriorproject.org

CHAPTER 1

DEEP YELLOW AND orange tongues of fire lapped up the sides of the old wooden structure, originally built in the late 1800's to service the railyards and shipping lines at the Columbia River in Portland's warehouse district. Once packed with frozen fish and sundries making their way from the Orient or Alaska, now the trendy area had sprouted galleries, high-end loft housing for young yuppies and artists, catering companies hosting exotic food trucks, eclectic restaurants that seemed to pop up and disappear with the same speed, dance clubs, and foreign movie theaters. It even had a live theater/playhouse converted from an old slaughterhouse by the same name.

The building was in a string of galleries that extended several blocks long on both sides.

Some housed artist collectives in a live-work environment, with the showrooms below. But like many of the old structures, this one was just a gallery, refurbished and benefiting from timeworn, wire-encrusted skylights thirty feet in the air, which gave the magic light that was so important to the paintings and artwork it housed.

But this night, midnight, it started in this building first, the fire like a wild snake, seeking out other places it could creep into cracks and overtake a new structure. The beautiful, polished white oak plank flooring buckled and popped nails as the fire traveled over the top like a tiny child's toy locomotive, leaving a fiery streak in its wake.

Glass broke as windows, one by one, burst open to the cold night air. Even the rain couldn't stop the spread, hissing and roaring like an angry animal ascending straight from Hell.

The paintings on the walls melted at first, their bright acrylic colors running down in bloody streaks past the canvas, over the walls, and onto the floor, pooling, igniting, and exploding in small balls of fire. Each picture was overtaken, and its demise was celebrated by the demands of the blaze. These works of art were abused, lit up for a few seconds, and then perished in flame.

One by one, the canvases dropped as their wires warped, as their frames charred, and the weight of the melted acrylic from the painting above it pushed them all down.

Within minutes, the entire building was engulfed, spreading to the one next to it and then another, until a paint factory caught and exploded. Oxygen temporarily removed from the air, a brief few seconds of darkness blanketed the landscape before the inferno came back to life with twice the strength.

If left unchecked, it would spread and consume the dozen or so warehouses all the way to the waterway. Sirens in the distance foretold this huge event would be coming to an end within the hour, already leaving behind black, smoldering partial walls while debris still ignited as new food for the fire.

And smoke. Thick, choking smoke so black the stars were invisible.

Diedre Gray was in shock when she got the call from the fire department liaison at one in the morning. Rushing to their bedroom window overlooking the river and downtown areas of Portland, she could see the blaze in the distance. She shared the gallery space with several other painters and a sculptor, but judging from the size and intensity of the blaze, she knew her work was all destroyed. And her paintings were the main draw of the gallery. She and the other artists held events in the space, all of them lovingly restoring and upgrading the building with the magical skylights.

Her heart broke, leaving only a thick, black, charred remnant of her former vibrant self. Twenty years of work, some pieces she never intended on selling, gone. Just gone.

Her husband stood behind her, holding her shoulders with his hands, while she wept. There were no words worthy of use. Nothing was going to stop her sobbing until she was good and done. The grieving process was beginning.

News reports flashed on their television as they listened for information. Her husband agreed with the department spokeswoman that going down there would be pointless and they would just be in the way. Since there wasn't expected to be any loss of life, pets, or items needing rescue, they'd let the professionals do their job undisturbed by their presence.

She called the other artists, one of whom had moved to San Francisco and was leaving the gallery, informing them of the sad news.

They continued to watch the reports. Earlier, a demonstration downtown in the financial district had left damaged vehicles and glass storefronts behind, including several fires which were quickly extinguished. Fire crews were blocked from entering certain blocks, and the police were relegated to pushing back the mob all the way to the grassy Dickenson Park in the center of the city, where they could be gathered up or dispersed. These demonstrations were now so common people didn't even pay attention as they re-routed their streets to avoid the confrontations.

Young people had poured out onto the sidewalk as one of the student housing units at Portland State downtown had been set ablaze. The newscaster wasn't sure what the demonstration was about, as no permit had been obtained and no spokesman had developed, which was also common these days.

The warehouse fire was deemed not connected, but arson was suspected. The protest crowd was trying to avoid the police and were headed that direction. Traffic and fire crews attempted to keep their work area cleared to further demonstrations, even onlookers, but were battling an angry crowd that seemed they wanted to burn down the whole city.

Deidre had cried so much she was now sitting in her flannel nightie in shock. Larry Gray brought her some of her favorite tea, and she sat, holding it, forgetting to sip, until he reminded her.

"Nothing we can do now, Deidre. What a shame."

"Why would they do that? The spokeswoman said it started with our building, Larry. Who would want to do that? Do you think it's related to downtown?"

"Makes no difference. A bank, a school dorm, a car dealership, a coffee shop, drug store—they all get hit these days. I just hope everyone gets out alive," he said, rubbing the back of her neck.

"This is unacceptable. This has to be stopped," she

whispered.

"It would be easier to move, Deidre."

"No. I'm going to stay and fight."

"But you don't even know who to fight. They just want to destroy. It's a statement that they want it all burned down, ruined. They won't be controlled."

"People have died, Larry, so they had the right to protest. Why can't they leave us alone to just do what we love?"

"It's evil. And the evil is growing."

And then she knew what she needed to do next. She would call her son, Navy SEAL Tyler Gray, in Coronado.

But she'd wait until morning.

CHAPTER 2

NAVY SEAL TYLER Gray heard screaming through the connecting wall from his two boys' bedroom. It was way too early on a Saturday morning. He'd been out late at a bachelor party for one of the tadpoles, new guy on SEAL Team 3, Oscar Ramos, and his head was killing him.

Besides, Kate usually jumped up first on these kinds of mornings to keep the peace between their three children. The boys had been fighting nonstop for weeks now. Oliver was the younger of the two boys, at five, and he competed in sports against his older brother, Grady, who was eight. He could nearly beat his older brother in a timed run and kick a soccer ball farther than most of the kids in his age bracket, as well as several years his senior. It wasn't something Grady tolerated well. Oliver made sure Grady was in a constant state of irritation and cut him zero slack. If Tyler had had a brother, he'd have been the same way.

But it made for a very noisy household.

Another scream erupted from their room, this time followed by a thump on the floor and then some serious crying.

He reached over to give Kate a hug, but then he remembered she had left before dark, driving up north to attend a catering class taught by a celebrity TV chef. So Tyler was in charge of all three kids all day.

He darted out of bed, shirtless but wearing red, white and blue boxers, and pushed the door to their bedroom so hard it banged against the wall and bent the door stop.

The crying stopped immediately.

Grady sat in the middle of the floor with a bloody nose. Oliver's right eye was going to be swollen shut soon.

"What the hell?" Tyler barked, barely able to change his language at the last minute to something more appropriate.

That's when he noticed Oliver silently set a large hardbound book down next to him, which had apparently been the weapon used to cause Grady's bloody nose.

"He hit me with a book," Grady shouted, pointing to the Three Musketeers book at Oliver's side. "He broke my nose!" he said through his bloody sniffles.

Tyler ran to the bathroom between their room and

Kendall's, grabbed a towel, and wet it down, bringing it back to Grady. Holding it up to his oldest son's nose, Tyler bent his head back.

"Keep this on it for a few minutes. Doesn't feel broken, Grady. Let's get the bleeding to stop, and then we'll sort this out."

Out of the corner of his eye, he noticed Oliver was slowly pushing the large book under his bed with his foot, removing the evidence.

"Ollie, you get your butt back on your bed, and gimme the book."

He did as he was told.

"Sorry, but he was pulling my hair. I had to stop him. He pushed me into the wall."

"I did not," Grady gurgled into the towel. "He called me a baby."

"Oliver, your brother is three years older than you. If he's a baby, what does that make you?"

"He wets the bed, and I don't," was Oliver's answer.

So there was the problem. Grady had recently had a bout of bedwetting, and Tyler and Kate had been scratching their heads to figure out what to do to make it stop. It was infrequent, but obviously embarrassing to Grady. Tyler was suspicious of most child psychologists, but Kate had been working on him to get him to agree to some counseling.

He was hoping Grady would just grow out of it. But

eight was pretty old for a bedwetter.

"That's not how we handle this sort of thing, Ollie. You need to apologize to your brother. And as for that shiner, you deserved it. If you can't take the heat, then keep your damned mouth shut, understand?"

"Yessir." Oliver hung his head.

From behind him, he heard the little voice of his two-year-old daughter, Kendall, "Daddy said a bad word."

She was standing in the doorway, holding her baby blanket and sucking her thumb.

"You're right, Sweetheart," he smiled and said to her. "Daddy made a mistake, and he's very sorry. It's okay to be angry but not okay to swear."

He stood, crossed the room to the doorway, and picked Kendall and her blanket up. Tickling her belly made her giggle. He sat her next to Oliver on his bed and tended to Grady.

The nose was going to be very red and swollen, especially up on the bridge, and he considered taking him to the emergency room to be checked but decided against it after examining him further. It would be a two- or three-hour ordeal, and he'd have to bring everyone with him. He also didn't want to expose the kids to the hospital crowd for fear they'd come home with a bug.

The bleeding had stopped. He grabbed the towel

and rinsed it in the bathroom sink.

The boys were still staring daggers at each other.

"Come on. Both of you say you're sorry, and let's shake on it." He watched as the two barely touched each other with the shake and mumbled their apology. It was as good as he was going to get.

He suddenly thought of something that might change the trajectory for the day.

"Who wants to go get pancakes?" he asked them.

The cheers he got were unanimous. He checked the time.

"You two get cleaned up. Grady, carefully brush your teeth and rinse your mouth, okay? And if I hear any arguing, the deal's off, and we get oatmeal downstairs. I have to change Kendall and get her ready."

THE HAPPY TIME Pancake House opened early. A Chinese family owned the business, sharing the kitchen with their Chinese restaurant, Happy Time Chinese, next door, which opened for lunch when the pancake house closed. Over the years he and Kate had been taking the kids there, they'd gotten used to the red lanterns and Chinese music playing in the background, but at first, eating pancakes to the ancient stringed orchestra had been distracting.

It was an acquired taste.

While they were waiting for their order to come,

Tyler's cell rang. It was his mother.

"Hey, Mom. You're up early."

"I hope I didn't wake you…"

"Not a chance. Kate's at a class so I'm taking the kids out for pancakes. What's up?" He suspected something important had happened.

"My gallery has burned to the ground, Tyler. It's just awful. What a mess."

"Oh my gosh. I'm so sorry, Mom. When did this happen?"

"Last night around midnight. They called to tell me it was fully engulfed. We watched it from our balcony. This morning, your dad and I went over early, but they wouldn't let us in. But there aren't any walls, and the roof caved in. Everything's destroyed. Gutted seven other buildings as well as damaged several others. A paint company exploded right behind us."

"Everyone okay?"

"One of the firefighters was taken to the hospital, but yes, everyone is okay. Nobody was in any of the buildings. Several people got out in time."

"I can imagine how you feel, Mom. You had a lot of paintings there as I recall. And—"

"I had just moved several pieces there to store them. They were my keepers, the ones I wanted to pass down to the family. Some of my favorites. And they're all gone, I'm sure of it."

"Well, I'm glad no one was hurt, except for the firefighter. Hope it wasn't serious."

"No, the news said he would be released."

"What caused the fire?"

"They suspect arson. But there was a protest downtown last night earlier. Several places were set ablaze. Nothing like this, though. The investigator and the news reports say there isn't a connection. I just don't know why anyone would want to burn down a gallery."

"You don't know that. Could have started elsewhere."

"No, they said it began with our building. We'll be told more later, they said."

"Maybe this is a sign, Mom. I've been asking you to move down to San Diego to be close to us. The kids would love seeing you. Now that Linda and the girls are down here too, it just makes sense to be where both your kids are. Dad could get a principal's job down here no problem. Or retire. I don't like what I'm hearing. I don't think it's safe there any longer."

"But we've been here our whole lives. We met here, went to college together, and started the gallery. My roots are here."

"Except now they're soot and smoke, Mom. Promise me you'll think about it."

"Your dad is just like you. No, we'll have to straighten out things here with the insurance, and then we'll see where we are. I'd like to be able to get inside the place."

"You won't be able to until it's safe. You don't want to interfere with the investigation, either, right?"

"Right."

Then Tyler heard her voice quiver and knew she was softly crying.

"What's wrong with Grandma?" asked Grady.

"I'll tell you in a minute. Eat your eggs first then the pancakes. Everyone, eat your eggs first," Tyler instructed his brood. He addressed his mother. "We've just been served, so I'm going to have to go. Is there anything I can do?"

"I was wondering, both your dad and I were wondering, if you could talk to the fire inspector and just get a feel for—"

"Look, you know I can't interfere."

"Yes, but you sort of represent the family. I guess you could call and talk to them on the phone, but I was hoping you could come up for a couple of days and help us sort out what has to be done."

"Well, I'm not trained in that. But if it will make you feel better, sure, I can try to come up. I won't be able to talk to Kate until tonight when she gets home, and I'll have to check with Kyle. You know I have to be careful not to step on any toes, and I don't know anything about fires, but if it will help you and Dad,

I'm willing. I am curious about why they think your building was the first one. Must have found something that led them to that conclusion. I would like to hear more about that."

"Oh, thank you, Tyler. It would be a great help to have you here."

Tyler spent the day cleaning up the mess in the boys' bedroom, washing sheets, and making sure the house was straight for when Kate got home. He called Kyle and got approval to take a couple of days off, since they weren't going to deploy for another couple of months, but there was a training coming up, preparing them for another trip to Mexico, possibly Central America as well.

He made a reservation for the one direct flight to Portland from San Diego, which he could cancel without penalty. He'd gotten the last seat and knew they would oversell the flight, so he'd get to the airport early tomorrow to make it.

He searched the internet news reports about the demonstrations that turned ugly in the downtown region and saw pictures of the warehouse fires, recognizing his mother's gallery roasting like a huge marshmallow.

It crossed his mind to contact Bryce Tanner and even perhaps Bone Frog Protection, an international security company who recruited former military, police, and rescue personnel for high-value hostage rescues. He wondered if they had any intel on groups who were involved with the violence.

Then he remembered the cautionary advice he'd gotten from Kyle and others. The first reports, just like the first reports of any military action, were always inaccurate. In an uncertain world, that was one thing he could count on.

As if sensing the trouble and danger to their grandmother, the kids were well behaved the rest of the day. They were seated at the dinner table when Kate arrived home, exhausted from the traffic and long drive.

He let the boys tell her about their fight, since she noticed the wounds, especially the shiner on Oliver's eye. Tyler added that everyone shook hands and apologized.

She smiled up at him. "Sounds like an ordinary day. Grady's nose is turning a little blue. Should we get it checked?"

"I think we should watch it. If you insist, I can do it tomorrow, but I was hoping to be able to go up to Portland to see Mom and Dad."

And then he told her about the fire. She agreed he should go.

As she sat down and Tyler served her dinner, little Kendall made sure she heard her news.

"And Daddy said a very bad word, Mama."

CHAPTER 3

KATE LOADED THEIR Suburban with the three kids, adding Tyler's duty bag, minus the weapons and rounds. He'd brought several sets of folded jeans and tee shirts, and one nice shirt and cotton pants with his leather shoes he hoped he didn't have to wear. They'd gotten used to wearing flip-flops between deployments in San Diego, and it always hurt to wear lace-ups or heavy boots. He told her he was usually medically treating blisters the size of his palm during their first few days overseas.

She and Tyler had talked until late in the evening what their future plans could be. It made sense for Mr. and Mrs. Gray to relocate to San Diego, but Tyler warned her that his mom was going to be resistant.

She answered, "I know she wants to be closer to the grandkids. Your dad can always find a good job down here. But he's almost seventy, Tyler. Don't you think he's considering retiring?"

Sitting next to her on the front seat, Tyler searched the windshield, thinking. "My parents have always done their own thing. You know they were hippies in college, right?"

"Oh yeah, we've talked about it. I think your folks went a little bit further than mine did, but it was the times. Your mom has never really grown out of that hippie phase. I mean, look at her paintings—"

And then Kate was reminded that most of her paintings were now destroyed in the fire. "Oh gosh, Tyler, I'm sorry."

"Well, it removes one root they have there in Portland. They spent so much time and money fixing up that place. Even though she loved it, now that it's gone, I'm just not sure my folks want to go through the whole thing again. I mean, it was one thing twenty years ago when they were a lot younger. Now, if Dad is going to retire, I don't think they have that much in savings. She does okay with her sales, but you know, I don't think they have the money."

"Well, you know a lot of artists up there live above their studios, and I, for one, would not be in favor of them selling the house on the hill and doing that. I think it's dangerous for them. So if that comes up, count me as a no. And I think your sister would feel the same."

"I think you're right. Linda is not really sure where

she wants to land after her last divorce. She can live anywhere since she's supporting herself with her writing now, but I think she's headed to Florida. Still looking for Mr. Rich Guy. Maybe she'll find him there. With her two kids in tow, I doubt Mom and Dad are really going to see their grandchildren very often. But it is what it is."

"You know, when I first met your folks, they were so lovey-dovey to each other. It was a little off-putting to be honest with you. I mean I never asked my parents how often they had sex, but your parents, hell, I think they have sex twice a day at least, right?"

Tyler threw his head back and laughed until they both heard their two boys unanimously shout out, "Ew," from the second seat behind them.

"Now you've done it, Tyler," she chuckled.

"I guess I have. And boy, if you're right about Mom and Dad, we've got to up our game, Kate. I can't have my seventy-year-old father outperform me in the bedroom."

"I doubt that's the case, Sweetheart," she said, giving him a sexy grin.

Tyler leaned over and placed a kiss on her cheek. "Later, Sweetheart, when I get home, I'm just going to show you. And that's all I'm going to say."

She turned the corner, following the signs to the airport.

"Do you think they'll rebuild then?" Kate asked him.

"I don't know. They seem to think they're in their twenties, that they'll be young hippies forever, live forever, and I don't know what it's going to take to change their minds. Maybe this is a good wake-up call for them. Maybe this will help them cut those ties, dig up their roots, and spread out a little bit. Maybe they will come down to San Diego. Although, it's going to be a lot more expensive."

"Maybe they could move in with us?" Kate asked. She wasn't excited about the idea, but she was willing to help at least until Deidre and Larry could get their bearings. "Just for a year or two, until they figure out what they want to do?"

"Well, I'll tell you one thing, if there's no insurance proceeds, their choices are going to be limited. And one of the first things I'm going to do is check their policy and make sure they get every penny that's coming to them. Insurance companies often try to scam unsuspecting homeowners into thinking they have less coverage than they have. I've heard stories."

"Yeah, I have too, Tyler."

"And if this is some kind of a crime investigation, it's probably going to delay things."

"I think it takes a month or two or maybe longer for the insurance company to settle up. They have to get prices and—"

"Well, the building structure probably wouldn't be a big deal, but those paintings, I just don't know how they'd value them. They're her paintings. They're probably going to say she could always duplicate them, which is stupid, but that's what they're going to say. They are worth probably more than the insurance is going to cover. But it all depends on how they insured them. I just hope to God my mom didn't let it lapse. She's known for being a little absent-minded with the bills now and then."

That worried Kate. Her silence seemed to be a red flag for Tyler.

"You okay?"

"You raise some worrisome points, Tyler. I didn't even think of all the questions I had about the fire and how they're going to go forward. I didn't even think about them not having proper insurance. And you're right, that does limit what they can do."

"I'm not going to worry about it until I know I have to. My biggest problem, my biggest job is going to be convincing my stubborn mother that she could paint down in San Diego. She just might not be painting a lot of trees, rose gardens, rivers, and woods. She might be starting a new chapter in her career, painting beach scenes, the Coronado Village area, landscaping around the little cottages down by the beach. I think she'd like it. I really do. It's a beautiful area, lots of color, and I think it would be good for her."

Kate agreed and added, "Maybe it'll be a new chapter for all of us."

At the drop off, Kate hugged Tyler at the same time the kids surrounded him. He picked up little Kendall, who was crying.

"Don't go, Daddy. I don't want you to go," she said, sniffling.

"Listen, Sweetheart. I'm putting you in charge! You watch your big brothers, and you keep track of how many times they argue, okay? It's your job to monitor them."

"Okay, Daddy."

"Before you know it, I'll be back."

She nodded her head as Tyler handed her back to Kate. The boys gave him one last leg squeeze. Kate kissed him hard on the lips, wanting to make a lasting impression. She watched him walk away, surrounded by their three children. That long sexy gait of his carried him away, as he slung the duty bag over his shoulder and disappeared into the bowels of the airport.

It was always the same. Each time, she wondered if it would be the last time she'd ever see him. She tried to soak up everything she could about watching his backside vanish into the crowds. In the meantime, she would pray, hold her breath more often as she thought about him, and attend to their three kids.

Like he'd said earlier, no reason to worry until there was something to worry about. Until then, the goal was to just live with gusto, pray for a tomorrow, and get ready for a stellar reunion with all the stars and stripes and the marching band. It was all about celebrating the now for as long and intensely as possible.

And never let fear, mistrust, or worry interfere with their love.

CHAPTER 4

H IS MOM AND dad met him at the Portland International Airport. When the plane left San Diego, it
finished its final ascent into the skies just about the
time it had to begin its decent. The flight was slightly
longer than an hour, and Tyler really didn't have much
opportunity to get properly settled before they were on
the ground.

"Great to see you, Tyler!" his mother said, grabbing
him and placing a big kiss on his cheek, while his dad
patted his back and waited his turn to give a hug.

"Boy, son, you bulked up. You lifting weights
again?"

"Oh, we kind of have a healthy competition going
on. I'm training some new medics, and I've been taking
them out for runs and showing them the ropes. They
think they can kick my butt, but at thirty-seven, I'm
still stronger than almost all of those guys in their early
twenties. I love showing them that, too, and since they

have to go through extensive PT, I've been doing it right alongside them. So yeah, I guess if I ever stopped being a SEAL, I could go do WWE or something."

Both his parents laughed. Tyler noticed his mother had dark circles under her eyes, and her cheeks looked a little gaunt. He knew she probably hadn't slept since the night of the fire.

"Let me take that," his dad said, grabbing Tyler's duty bag.

"Nah, Dad, I got it. I know you can do it, but let me take this."

"All right, but just so you know, I work out too."

Tyler stopped and examined him from head to toe and back up to his head again. "God damn, Dad. You have been working out. I can tell."

"Well, probably not like you, but we go to the senior center."

"I do Aquarobics while he does the machines," his mother added.

"Good for you. You know what they say, either use it or lose it. None of us are getting any younger."

Downstairs, they walked through the pedestrian traffic area, over to the parking garage, where his father had driven his vintage 1969 Volkswagen bus. It was his father's prized possession and was inoperable during most of Tyler's growing up years. But his parents had lots of stories about that van, the places it went, and the romantic escapades his parents used to have. As a young kid, it used to embarrass him. He figured that's where his sister got her jive to write romance novels, although she never wrote about the sixties or seventies.

The moss green colored van was shiny, having been freshly polished, and stored in the garage. It had a cream white top with little moon roof windows along the ceiling, and the original plastic straps instead of armrests on the doors in the second and third rows. His father had souped it up a bit with a new engine several years ago, but during the first years they had it, the van was legendary for holding up a stream of twenty to thirty cars as it tried to climb the hills leading to their house.

"Would you look at this thing? It's perfect still. You must be out there every day washing and waxing it," Tyler remarked.

"He loves it more than me, I think," said his mother.

"Aw, I call foul. Deidre, you know that's not right. The only reason I've kept this van is because of the wonderful memories we made in it. And still make in it too, I might add." He winked at his son.

Tyler put his hands over his eyes and then covered his ears and shook his head. "La, la, la, la, la, la. I didn't hear that. I don't want to hear that. TMI, TMI."

When he looked up at his folks, they were beaming

from ear to ear. He hoped that, as the years went by, he and Kate could have that kind of a relationship. His father adored his mother, allowing her to paint and be the free spirit that she was in her heart, while he was the main bread winner as a school principal.

He was one of the most revered members of the Portland public school system and had passed up the opportunity to become superintendent several times, because he didn't want to be removed from the classroom, which is where he developed the love of teaching. A very tall and handsome man with bright azure blue eyes, his white hair and salt-and-pepper beard made for a striking combination. He often disarmed people just by the way he intently studied them, and his casual, conversational dialect was pleasant and often welcoming.

Of all the people in Portland, Tyler could not understand how anybody in their right mind would ever wish either one of his parents harm. He figured the arson must have been an opportunity crime, someone who wanted to make a statement. He knew it couldn't be personal.

His dad fired up the old bus, and they headed out from the parking garage, twisted around several turns, and finally made it to the freeway for their approach to the hills overlooking Portland where the house was located. Before he turned to start climbing the road,

Tyler stopped him. "Can you drive me by the warehouse?"

"Well, we haven't been given the okay yet. They are still doing their investigation, removal of evidence, and some minor cleanup. The city has to make the streets and the surrounding areas passable. So there've been road crews out there, and they've had it barricaded off. But we can go try if you want. Is that okay with you, Deidre?" He looked at his wife and asked.

"Doesn't hurt to try, Larry." She turned to address Tyler. "They might not allow it. So don't get your hopes up."

As Mr. Gray turned away from Palatine Road, which wound up the hill, he headed toward the Columbia River, which soon became a mixed-use neighborhood of residence-converted flats, businesses, and industrial warehouses.

Tyler asked, "So have they told you anything new?"

"Not a thing. We're just letting them take their time, do what they need to do. We don't want to get in their way, but yeah, it would be nice to know. My insurance office already has the claim. I'm supposed to get a call and an appointment in one to two days, they said. He said he was going to try to go over and take some pictures, but I doubt they're going to let him in."

"Well, Dad, you want to be there when he takes his pictures and does the inspection. And you want to overhear the conversation he has with the fire marshal or inspector. You just don't want any surprises, okay? One of the things you have to realize is that these adjusters make their money by keeping the claims low. One of our SEAL buddies had parents who had a fire, and the adjuster came over the next day and wrote them a check, which was great, except that it only covered about a third of the expenses of rebuilding their house. They learned too late that, had they not accepted that check, they would've been able to apply for more and were entitled to quite a bit more. So don't jump on everything just because they offer you some money."

"Yes, our neighbor told us that as well. Funny thing, our insurance agent said that the first offer is usually the best offer," his mother said with a sly smile.

Tyler shook his head. "That's BS, Mom. You know that, right?"

"We do now. Thanks, Son," said his dad.

Several blocks away from the fire scene, the streets were blocked off with bright orange barricades. Several of Portland's police and public safety group manned the barricades and only allowed rescue and city workers inside. The place looked like an anthill to Tyler, there were so many vehicles driving around. People were consulting in small clusters of two or three, power crews were restoring telephone and electrical lines, and even the gas company was there. A large debris box had been ordered and sat right in front of Tyler's parents' former warehouse. There were several other debris boxes further down the street until he could see barricades at the end, about eight or ten blocks away.

They were stopped by a policeman who leaned into the car, his arm on the windowsill. "Can I help you?"

Tyler noticed the policeman was searching the inside of the vehicle, probably trying to assess whether or not the passengers had weapons or some kind of contraband.

His dad spoke up. "We're the Grays, and the warehouse over there is—was—my wife's gallery that belongs to us, or used to anyway. My son is up here from San Diego, and we wanted to see if we could just walk around the outside a little bit, not interfere with your work at all but just see how bad it is. We haven't been able to do that yet." Tyler watched the policeman frown.

Then he pulled out a list of owners' names and addresses and put a check mark next to theirs.

"I have you on the list. Can I see some identification, please?"

Both of Tyler's parents reached out the window with their IDs. Tyler brought out his special forces' ID and handed it to the policeman as well.

"Oh, so we have ourselves a regular hero here. Is

that it?"

"Not really, sir," said Tyler.

At the same time, Tyler's folks agreed with the policeman. His mother added, "He sure is. Very proud of him, sir. He's up here from San Diego to just help us sort this out."

"Well, I can allow you to park down the street in the makeshift parking lot, but you're going to have to walk, and you can't really enter onto the property. You can just stay in the street and take a look at it from the street level. I can't let you go into the back or walk through the building. And if a delivery or energy or rescue truck shows up, you're to give him complete right away, is that understood?"

"Thank you, sir," Tyler barked back at him from the second seat. "We appreciate that. No worries here. We're not going to interfere with anything."

"Well, Son, I figured as much. Be sure to check back with me before you go, so I can mark you off. Now, if you go down about a block and a half, you'll see several cars parked in a row. Please park right behind that first line of cars, and I'll meet you back here as soon as you can make it down the street."

"Sir," Tyler asked him again. "Is there a senior fire inspector or incident commander available here? Do you see anybody in position of leadership here that we might be able to speak with and ask questions of?"

The policeman scanned the area, squinting as he looked farther down the street. "I don't see them. They were here earlier for a briefing. We had news media here, of course, as you might imagine. The mayor was here, and I understand the governor's going to be here later on today. But no, I don't see him right now."

"Thanks, Man."

"No problem, Son."

They drove to the parking lot, Mr. Gray not quite obeying the policeman. Instead of parking in the grassy field, which was dusty with whirls of sooty debris blown all over, covering windshields and everything else in front of them, he went an extra block and parked at a gas station that was closed. They left the car there, locking it up.

The policeman let them through, and slowly, they walked over broken glass, pieces of metal strips, partially charred tree branches, sooty leaves, and some concrete rubble and fallen trees. Several of the rescue vehicles had driven over these, so scoring the whole area were dusty tire tracks of the engines and city vehicles.

The trees were all gone. The denuded fire site made the burned city blocks look like a scene in hell. The fire tended to equalize every color that previously inhabited this area, and it had been a fairly colorful area too. But now everything was black or dark gray; nothing in this several block long area survived. They did find a couple birds that somehow had gotten trapped in the smoke, and a squirrel tried to hop in front of them, appearing to be slightly injured. Its tail was scorched on one side, knocking his balance off.

"Was anybody living here at the time?" Tyler asked them.

"They said not. I know there were some lofts farther down they were working on, but I don't think they were ready to go on the market yet," his mother said. "They're standardizing this whole area and changing some of their zoning requirements, so my understanding is that the project took a lot longer than they expected to fully develop. And a lot of the people who own warehouse space here weren't really excited about a large yuppie population moving in. But what can you do?" she said, shrugging her shoulders.

When they stood in front of what would've been the entrance to the warehouse, they noticed the plastic fencing that had surrounded the property had melted and looked like marshmallow sauce on an ice cream sundae. No windows or doors or anything of any significant-sized timber remained. It was all a pile of ash, long ribbons of grey reaching to the sky. Everything was soaked, flooded. Several rolls of straw that Tyler had recognized from flooding on freeways in the San Diego area were diverting the black sooty water from the lot and down into the storm drain and gutters. The air still had an acrid bitter scent to it, even with the wind and promise of further rains. It would take weeks before that would go away, he knew.

He watched his mother stare at what used to be her beautiful gallery. Suddenly, her tears erupted over her lower lids and silently trickled down her cheeks. Tyler thought about all the work and the love she had put into those paintings that now were gone forever. He decided to find something positive and not dwell on the bad.

"Mom, at least you weren't here working late. I know you like to do that sometimes, so count your lucky stars."

"He's right, Deidre," said Tyler's dad.

"You're healthy. You aren't injured. This is just stuff. I know it's horrible to think about it that way, but the finger of God touched this place, and he decided you had too much. It was time to get rid of it. I think he knew you were going to putz around with it and it would take you a long time to decide what to keep, what to store. So he gave you a hand. He just touched the building, and he took it all."

As he said this, he noted his mother gasped and inhaled sharply, shaking and trying to grasp how this could be a good thing. Maybe he'd gone too far. Maybe she wasn't ready.

He wrapped his arm around her shoulders, placed his cheek next to hers, and whispered, "It's all good, Mom. There's a new future out there. And I'm going to help you find it."

She let him hold her for several minutes before she could respond. He once again felt the frailty of her body, yet she stood firm, heels dug in, not wavering. Her steel and resolve began to show. He withdrew his embrace, allowing her the freedom to build on what she'd started.

"I just have such a hard time saying goodbye to so much. I have never lost so much. I feel so violated. Just devastated. Oh, I wonder how we are going to deal with all this, this hurt, all these decisions we must make. I just, I'm—I'm overwhelmed. I think once I get past that, I'll cry myself to sleep for about two weeks. And then, I think I'll be all right. But this, this is not what I ever expected would happen. And I'm still asking myself why."

He was proud of her, of her strength. His dad's loving arms encircled her, whispering encouragements, patting her back, and giving her little kisses at the side of her face. She was holding up, all things considered, well.

"Mom, this isn't anything you can't recover from. Like I said, God took all this stuff away, so you could start a new life. The only thing we need to figure out is what that's going to look like. But thank goodness you're okay."

CHAPTER 5

KATE BROUGHT THE kids home after dropping Tyler off at the airport, so they could work on their chores and Grady could finish his homework. Oliver had books to read but no formal homework yet. She set Kendall down to watch some animal movies while her two older children busied themselves with their work.

She put her notes from the catering class in their office, stored in a binder along with all the other research she'd been doing. They had considered several different options as far as their future—a future after Tyler left the team. She knew he was beginning to feel they had reached that point. All the SEAL wives knew either from age, injury, family priorities, or sheer exhaustion would force their men to leave the job that they all knew was perfect for them, tailor-made for these strong warriors and big-hearted guys. Tyler had put in more time than most, since the average was a "one and done" tour of six years.

At one point, they'd seriously considered moving back to Sonoma County after his retirement, but since the kids were involved in so many San Diego activities and were used to playing with the other SEAL kids, they thought it would be too disruptive for the family. Now with the possibility of some kind of different future for Tyler's parents, they would have to consider things they hadn't before, including buying a house large enough for all of them to live in.

But Kate discovered she'd developed a deep love of entertaining and wanted to try her hand at setting up a catering company or a lunch wagon that served high-end office workers downtown and in Old Town. She envisioned making healthy sandwiches, soups, and salads.

With the heavy Hispanic population in San Diego, there was no shortage of taco trucks. Kate hoped to also have a full menu of ethnic foods but wanted to try her hand at cooking them in alternative ways: low-calorie, meatless, keto-type recipes and juices.

The class she had taken in Los Angeles on Saturday had really piqued her interest. She'd been dreaming about her new business venture, making it almost impossible for her to sleep. So while Tyler tossed about in bed, focused on his parents and the fire, Kate had dreamed about her future. Was this wrong, uncaring, or too self-centered?

No, she thought. It was her way to safeguard the future for all of them. She was happiest building things, creating a sustainable income stream they could rely on, and planning something that she enjoyed.

She decided to give Devon Dunn a call since Devon and her husband owned a winery and lavender farm up in her old stomping grounds, Sonoma County. They operated it as a wedding center, which was by far the most profitable portion of the business. Kate liked the idea of perhaps purchasing a piece of property down in San Diego or the Coronado area. She could also picture a larger home with a beautiful garden setting where she could Airbnb the property and make it a destination wedding venue. Since their budget would be limited, she considered that they'd probably have to look for heavy fixers.

Devon picked up on the first ring.

"Kate, how's it going?"

Kate could hear activity in the background. It sounded like she had a crowd and had picked up the phone in their large rental hall.

"Did I catch you in the middle of an event?"

"Well, yes, but I have a couple of minutes before I must be front and center. Hosting a silent auction and benefit luncheon for one of the private schools, raising money for their sports program. So, go ahead, I'm all yours for about five."

"Thanks. I'm doing well, although Tyler has flown up to Portland to be with Larry and Deidre—I don't know if you've heard, but their gallery burned down Friday night. They suspect it's arson, but there were also quite a few demonstrations in the downtown area, so we don't really know whether this was a satellite demonstration or just troublemakers. But the fire inspector is certain that it is arson. And it took out another eight or ten buildings, even a paint company."

"This is the first I'm hearing of it. Nick has been to that gallery. I think they even might have had a work party before we got together. I'm so sorry, Kate. They must be devastated. And she has such beautiful paintings. Did she lose very many?"

"Yes, I believe she said it was around forty. Over half of them were paintings she never intended to sell, just kept for herself or to pass down to the family. That's the most heartbreaking part of it. And also, they loved putting together that center, housing other artists, and having events there. Kind of like what you do except on a much smaller scale and for the artsy crowd. It's part of their lifestyle, and now we don't know what their future holds. We don't know if they have the money to rebuild or if they even should. There're lots of decisions we're making."

"I have been hearing some of these reports about Portland. What a shame. Such a fun city to visit. All those quaint little shops and the bookstore. What's it called?"

"Powell's?"

"Yes, that's it. Great restaurants. Lots of churches, as I recall, and movie theaters. Beer halls. It's a city that even in the rain it's fun to be out walking in. Lovely rose gardens, wild rhododendrons, and views of the beautiful Columbia river, all the river traffic. Now there's crime and homelessness spiraling out of control. Not enough personnel and police and fire to protect the public. I don't know—I just don't know if I want to go see it and experience what's been happening up there lately. The news pictures are horrible. Do you feel safe?"

"Not any more, Devon. Tyler's been working on his parents to move down to San Diego."

Devon was quiet on her end of the phone. Finally, she added, "So I guess you are no longer considering coming up here and helping us with the winery?"

They'd had serious discussions about buying into Nick and Devon's complex, perhaps moving there and becoming partners. The fire had changed everything.

"Well, that's partly what I wanted to talk to you about. I think that scenario is probably a long shot at this point. But we don't really know. I've been taking some classes and researching the catering business. I kind of like the idea of starting a food truck and creating healthy foods, an alternative to all the lunch wagons we have here. Some of the big office buildings who can't all go out to lunch or bring in their food would love gourmet, healthy foods, juices, maybe soups. I really think I could make a go of it. What do you think, Devon?"

"Well, I love to cook, but I don't think having a catering truck or a lunch wagon would be anything I'd want to do, but who knows? I think it's a good idea. And there are probably a lot of very health-conscious people down there. You might have a winner there, Kate. Although, I still think having a place, an event site, and then doing catering would make you more money. But that's just me."

"You think so? We can't do anything like what you have."

"We have the winery, and we have the lavender farm, but mostly because Nick inherited it from his sister. Otherwise, I'm not sure we could have pulled it off. A tragedy-turned-miracle. But, oh my gosh, it's so much work. It's wonderful work. And it's been good for the whole family to be involved, but the events and the ecotourism we're doing now pays much better. It's sort of an expensive hobby, I guess, the winery production is. Zak and Amy up in Healdsburg probably are doing a little bit better as far as that goes. But they're smack in the middle of Dry Creek Valley, world famous for outstanding wines and sort of on the highway for the wine tourism industry. We've had our setbacks as far as the winery and the lawsuits. But I think we're on firm ground now. But expanding the winery is so expensive, and it's hard to calculate market trends. You plant and then don't have a decent harvest for seven years!"

"Ouch! I get it."

"But tell me how you came to this idea of a catering truck."

"Well, when I was sitting in class and they were going over business models, profit and loss and proforma statements, and all the different food-related businesses that one could try, I just got really excited about the idea. And it's not anything I ever expected to do."

"It's a calling. It really is. Very artistic, in a way, like gardening. You don't know what you'll get, but you love experimenting with things, making things beautiful. Think of the people you'd serve, who I think would spend good money to eat more healthy. Not everyone is satisfied with a deep green milkshake for lunch!"

Kate had to laugh. "And all the burping and farting afterwards that would drive the office batty."

"You're right about that."

"But seriously, Devon, I'd love to come up and shadow you for a while. Maybe bring the kids if it isn't too much? We could come up during Thanksgiving or

Easter break when they're all out of school?"

"Sure, anytime. School breaks are some of our busiest times. I'll put Oliver and Grady to work. Customers love seeing kids in these events. It's great training for customer service skills, and I'm sure Nick could put them to good use out in the fields too. Depending on when you come, we could be doing pruning or the crush or tying off some of the vines, weeding, I think they'd enjoy driving up and down the rows in the tractor with Nick and the girls."

"Oh, I think they'd love it. Kendall is going to be a bit of a handful, but I think she'd enjoy it too."

"Do you have any specific dates in mind?" Devon asked her.

"No, not yet. I want to wait until Tyler gets home to finish the discussions we've started. Don't want to plan something he's not completely behind."

"Sure. That's wise."

"And now, we have to talk about his parents and see what is what about their insurance and whether or not they're going to rebuild. It may be that, if they have enough of a settlement, they could buy their own place down here. But prices are rather high compared to Portland. There's just a lot of things we have to consider. But I mainly wanted to tell you that I'm interested and I'd love it if you could mentor me and show me the ropes, especially around the Airbnb."

"I'd be happy to, Kate. And you don't even have to come up here. I can show you everything I do with a Zoom call. You could get your computer out, and I could help you get set up online at some of the places I advertise in. It's really very simple. The time-consuming part is being connected to your computer and always making sure you get back to people right away. That's where I think a lot of businesses fail."

"Well, I'm glad to hear things have settled down and are going well. I hope we can make it a family trip. I know Tyler would love to talk to Nick about his detachment. It's a big question in his mind, whether he could find something he loves as much as being on that team. We all know that the more times they deploy, the greater the likelihood they'll get injured or hurt or possibly worse. We always worry about that, don't we?"

"Oh, I remember those days. I probably wasn't the most supportive wife. I think Kyle still blames me for Nick retiring so soon. But it was the right choice. No way could I handle this by myself. And I still sell real estate as well. With the girls, the center, the winery, the lavender farm, and all the advertising, invoicing, and personnel issues I have to take care of, Nick winds up monitoring and working with the seasonal employees. It's an eighty-hour week for each of us. I just don't think there would've been a way for us to survive after all those lawsuits and problems with the neighbor unless he was fully detached. It was the right choice for us. But I'm sure Nick would love to talk to Tyler about it. It's a big decision. I know Nick misses the guys terribly."

Kate agreed. "You know, I think if we stayed in the Coronado San Diego area, Tyler may not feel so bad about the detachment."

"Yes, but there's the other side of that too. He'll see all his former teammates getting together and talking about their missions, and he's no longer a part of it. That could be frustrating as well. There's a lot of things to consider. Does he have any idea of what he wants to do other than the catering gig?"

"He says he'd like to help me. I think he could do anything he set his mind to. I'm just glad he's going to allow me to try something. And we'll have to wait and see how everything shakes out. But I'm so lucky that at least he's considering doing a project with me."

"Well, you know my opinion of these guys—they're the best of the best. And just because they're no longer on the teams, that ethos and that way of looking at the world and the way they treat people doesn't go away. I'd say you've got the best of both worlds if he wants to help you. I'd let him come on up here and explore it in earnest. And, Kate, I will do my very best to make it look fun and to enable him to fully engage. That would be my honor."

They ended the call with Kate agreeing to keep Devon and Nick informed and to touch base more often.

Next, Kate gave her mother a call, catching up on things the children were doing. And then she brought up the gallery fire in Portland.

"Oh dear, I saw the riots on the news, but I didn't know it had spread to their area. Deidre must be heartbroken," her mother said. "I just don't know what I'd do if something like that happened to us. Have they determined what caused the fire?"

"The fire inspector thinks it's arson. And it started at their warehouse and moved on down the street. They were able to stop it eventually, but it did a lot of damage to the neighborhood. Tyler's up there now going over all the insurance information and helping them file paperwork. At least he wants to be involved in talking with the adjuster. He's a bit anal about that score."

"I think that's a good idea. I'm glad he's able to and wasn't overseas. That should be a lot of help to them. What do you think they'll do?"

"You mean, will they rebuild?" Kate asked.

"Yes, do you think they'll build another gallery or maybe construct apartments or something else on that land? What do you think?"

"Tyler's dad is going to be seventy next year, and

he's past retirement age, but he really likes what he's doing, and the district isn't enforcing it, so I think if they were to do anything drastic, he'd probably retire. Then they might have some additional choices. Tyler and I would love to have them come down here, so they could be closer to the grandkids."

Her mother went quiet then continued. "Oh, I envy that. We're just not ready to make that kind of a move, but it would be nice to be closer to you. I don't know if your dad will ever retire. He's really driven."

"We're just thinking about everything." Kate felt the need to change the subject.

"And on another note, I went to a class in Los Angeles on Saturday. It's a series of lectures about forming a food industry business, like for people wanting to do catering, specialty restaurants, bakeries, or setting up some kind of a lunch truck. And the idea really intrigues me. I'm seriously thinking I'd like to try that."

"A lunch wagon. Really?"

"Yeah. What do you think?"

"I think you'd do great with that, Kate. You're such a good cook, and I know you'd enjoy doing catering, but it's a lot of work. I thought you were considering moving back up here, helping out with Nick and Devon's winery."

"We were. Still might. And you're right. It is a lot of work. But now things have shifted slightly. It might be hard on the kids to uproot them. I'd like to do what Nick and Devon do, but do it down here, along with the truck. Mom, there are so many possibilities. Now I want to fully explore all of them! Probably not on such a grand scale like they do, but maybe purchase something in need of work, fix it up, and create a venue. Make a wedding center out of it, create beautiful, lush gardens, and do the catering around that. Possibly rent the house out for international travelers and do a modified Airbnb with catering as an option."

"Wow, your head is really spinning."

"I got my eyes opened at this seminar. Tyler and I have talked, and he's open to the idea of maybe helping me. But nothing's set in stone yet. And we certainly have to figure out what his parents are going to do first."

"You know my theory about all that, Kate." Her mother began to sound stern.

Here comes the lecture.

"You should put yourselves first. Don't change your plans because of Tyler's parents. Of course you're wonderful to consider that, but you have to live your lives. They've had a wonderful life, but yours is just at the beginning stages. Those kids are going to grow up fast, Kate. If it's something you could do together, I don't see how Tyler could stay on the teams."

"No, you're right. He's considering not re-upping.

He's thirty-seven. It's time. It's time for somebody else to be a Boy Scout."

Her mother laughed. It warmed Kate's heart to hear that. She wished her mother was closer and was able to spend more time with her three children, but as she so aptly said herself, she was pursuing their own dreams, and right now, staying in Santa Rosa was what they wanted to do.

"Mom, I have to run, but I just wanted to let you know, and I'll update you as soon as I have some news. If you think of anything that would be helpful in dealing with the insurance company—I know Dad has had to deal with insurance companies for his business—we'd be grateful."

"I surely will. How's your sister Gretchen been doing? She still enjoying San Diego?"

"You would think with all the news, she'd feel she got out of Portland in time. But you're not going to believe this, Mom. She's actually thinking of moving back. Trace is also thinking of detaching from the teams, but they're just in the early stages of looking at it. She never sold her house there on the hill. I don't know why she'd want to move back there, but she's considering it. And I guess Trace has an offer from a company where a lot of the employees are former SEALs or Special Forces guys. That's life. Things change."

"I don't have to remind you that if you ever wanted to do your catering business here in your hometown in Sonoma County, your dad and I would help as much as we could. Just let us know."

"Thanks, Mom. Love you."

"I love you ten times more, Kate."

CHAPTER 6

AS TYLER'S DAD drove back through the warehouse neighborhood, rounding the damage site by two or three blocks away and looping down to the waterfront, he could see the homeless encampments. These camps encroached on the patios of restaurants getting ready to serve late lunch/early dinner, small business manufacturing companies and stores where employees would have to thread between a line of tents with the required thirty-six inches apart from each other, which was the law. He saw a group of school children coming home from one of the local elementary schools, walking past derelicts and drunks, one little boy even pushing a syringe into the gutter with his tennis shoe. It broke Tyler's heart that there were so many addicted, hurting people. It also broke his heart that so many innocent people were forced to be part of this community. He had to say something.

"Geez, Dad. I'm not so sure I want you driving.

Can you pull over and let me get behind the wheel for a bit?"

"Tyler, we've been putting up with this for several years now. They don't really care about me. They're going after expensive cars."

"Dad! This *is* an expensive car. Have you priced it lately?"

Tyler's mother looked over at her husband, "He's right, Larry. Why don't you let him drive?"

Tyler could tell his dad was under stress, because he never swore. But this time he let out a string of words he'd never heard him speak before. Rather than making note of it, he ignored it, opened the door, and traded places with the older man. That relieved Tyler's own worry and tension, but just a little.

"I had no idea things had gotten this bad. And, Mom, you were coming down here at night by yourself?"

"No, Silly. Larry would come with me. Or I'd meet one of the other artists down here. I would go out, have a cigarette in the backyard, and watch the sculptor throw some pots on the wheel. He worked out in the backyard at night, even in the light rain. We just didn't think anybody would be interested in our property. We were always kind to these people."

From behind the seat, Tyler's dad leaned over to him. "She brings sandwiches down for the guys that are on the corner asking for work or food. She brings them chocolate milk sometimes, and you know she's nice to them. We aren't the problem here."

The scene was all too familiar to Tyler. Should he tell them about how many innocent people were being abused all over the world? He just didn't expect to see it in the United States. And it really bothered him. There was something happening that was eating away at the very fabric and soul of the country.

"It's always that way with people who prey on innocent people. I understand why they're trying to make a living by panhandling here. Housing is expensive, and if they're a mess medically and we don't have hospitals or housing for them, they're going to want to stay on the street. Besides, I think a lot of them trust the street better than they trust our own government to set up something for them. But there's an element I can see here that's growing, based on all the tags I'm seeing on the buildings. Some young punks have moved in, muscling for space and control. I see it in how they look at me when I drive past them. This isn't a healthy environment at all. In fact, I'll bet if you really got into trouble here, it would take quite a while for the police to show up. In that amount of time, you might be dead, both of you."

He looked in his rearview mirror and made eye contact with his dad. He didn't flinch but stared right into his eyes. He was hoping his dad would take it to heart.

"What you are saying is we should only come down here in daylight, not at night?" his mother asked him.

"Mom, and this is the God's honest truth, I don't ever want to see you down here, especially by yourself, at any time of the day. I had no idea it looked like this. I feel like I've been living under a rock. This is horrible. This is a war zone. And I think I'm qualified to tell you what one looks like."

Tyler's father inserted himself into the conversation.

"It's only gotten bad the last couple of years since the pandemic, Tyler. It's just everybody's so stressed and city services are maxed out. We're the lucky ones. We have a house that's free and clear. We had this nice gallery. I've got a good job, and your mom makes money on her paintings and teaching. At the time, this was all we could afford as far as a large warehouse building. But, Tyler, I hear what you're saying, and maybe we should consider when we rebuild to relocate in a better neighborhood."

"Well, that would be a start. I want to see what the rest of Portland looks like and I want to see what your neighborhood looks like now. Is it my imagination or has everything just gone downhill?"

"You haven't been here for, I think, over two years,

Tyler. No one has been doing much traveling," his mother said. "We're just digging ourselves out as a city from the pandemic.

"Except that's not true. I've been traveling. I've been going to lots of places. There's no sense of safety here. There's no organized protection. They had more police guarding the barricade to keep looters out of the fire site than I see in the rest of this district. Honestly, I'm surprised that there isn't more of an objection to the way this is being handled."

"Well, you know our political views, and with my family's deep roots in the Quaker community, we thought we were helping by non-violently just going about our own business. We thought that would help the community better than to do anything else. We were investing in the city's future. Other than that, there really isn't anything we can do."

"You can vote, right?"

"Tyler," his dad said from behind him, "we aren't into social action—"

"Dad, voting is not social action. Voting is making your voice heard. And no, I'm not saying I want you to protest or march or do an anti-march protest to what they're doing. I just want you to help this neighborhood by voting in the people who will keep you protected. And it has nothing to do with politics. It has nothing to do with any political party. It's just wrong.

They don't have Republicans or Democrats in Nigeria, Venezuela, or the Caribbean. They have different names for their different parties. That's not the problem. It's the lack of people being willing to step up and protect the innocent."

Tyler's chest was shaking. He was so angry. All of this had been going on for the past couple of years, and he had been completely unaware of it, wouldn't have known about it until something like the fire happened. He kicked himself for not checking on his parents more often. He was certainly going to check in with the Bone Frog Group, a private security and protection company. This part of the States was going to start looking like what he'd seen in Brazil, where women and children went shopping in blacked out Suburbans with bulletproof windows and doors, accompanied by armed guards with semi-automatic rifles. That wasn't the country he expected to see here, and he didn't want it to be the future of Oregon or anywhere.

He gripped the steering wheel and softly apologized. "I have friends who gave their lives so that we could be safe in this country. It feels like such a waste when I see this. There is no excuse for it. I can't insert myself here because we're constrained against that. But somebody's got to do something, and I don't like the signs. I really don't want you to rebuild here. Please, if you can just promise me that, I'll shut up."

"I guess we should have told you. But honestly, we thought it would get better now that people are going back to work and trying to reconnect with their lives. The pandemic appears to be subsiding, hopefully."

Tyler looked into the face of his mother and realized that she was trying to help him, but there wasn't a blasted thing she could do.

And she didn't even realize it.

The downtown financial district of Portland was cold and windy, the sun being blocked by a combination of rain clouds and tall skyscrapers. It felt to him like San Francisco, without the beautiful blue San Francisco Bay and sunlit, colorful bridges spanning it. Again, there were gang tags, streets littered with trash, and several businesses in a once-thriving downtown that were boarded up. Some posters advertised a resistance movement touting all kinds of different ideologies and theories that Tyler didn't pay any attention to. But although it wasn't as bad as the warehouse district, it still didn't paint a very secure picture to him.

He began to understand the enormity of the problem. He knew he was going to work very hard to get his parents out of the city and get them somewhere where he could check on them and where he felt they'd be safer. He just wouldn't be able to live with himself if something horrible happened to them. Here they were exposed. They probably didn't realize it because the changes had come on so gradually they didn't notice or told themselves it still wasn't as bad as it was elsewhere. It was the frog in the water scenario. By the time the frog realized the water was boiling, it was too late to save himself.

He took Palatine Boulevard winding up the hill in switchbacks until he got to the top. There was a large hospital there, and just down the street from it, facing the Columbia River, was their house.

His mother had always chosen bright colors to paint it, and this year, the color seemed to be golden yellow. It had white trim on the extensive porch. The steps were painted white on their risers, all the trim and the handrails were white, and it looked like they'd reroofed the house with green asphalt shingles.

Parking the van in the garage out back, he followed his mother in through the kitchen door. She gave him a hug as he dropped his duty bag.

"Well, I guess that wasn't exactly the kind of welcome you expected. I'm so sorry, Tyler. I really should have thought about warning you."

"Mom, it's not about me. I'm worried about you and Dad. I'm worried that you're not worried. But look, let's just forget about all this for right now. I think what I'd like to do is lie down, take a little nap, maybe get up, and take a shower. I have a few calls I need to make, and then I'm all yours the rest of the day and the evening."

"When do you want me to schedule the insurance agent to come over and speak to us?" his dad asked, coming in through the doorway.

"Well, I guess the adjuster is probably the one you want to speak to first."

"Oh, our agent says we can go through him. He said it's a very long, detailed process, and he could help streamline it. Grease the skids so to speak," his dad said.

"I'm not sure that's the case. I really want to talk to the adjuster. What the adjuster writes down is what you're going to get, and if he writes down the wrong things, then it's going to make a difference. But one thing you can do is get out your policies and let me look them over when I get done with my nap. Okay?"

"Fair enough."

"I've got to call Kate and let her know I arrived safely, that I've seen the property. Then I have to check in with my LPO just to let him know also what I see here. And finally, I have a couple other friends in the area I'd like to call. Just to touch base. It's been a long time since I've seen them."

"You go right ahead, Son," said his father. "We'll give you some privacy. Come down when you're ready."

He dashed up the stairs, like he had done as a child growing up. He went to the second door on the right, which was his old room, and discovered things had not changed since the last time he'd been here. He had brought Grady to a soccer tournament up in Portland, and the two of them had spent the night in his old room, which impressed Grady no-end. Tyler's trophies were still lined up along the windowsill and in the cabinet his dad had to make to house all the later ones, which kept getting bigger and bigger as his wins increased. Grady was just starting out and had visions of becoming a great soccer player like his dad. It had been a fun father-son event. Tyler let him take home one of the trophies to remember the trip by. Of course, he chose the biggest one, parading it through the airport on their way home.

He stripped out of his clothes and jumped in the shower, feeling that if he could just wash the stench of the fire, the travel, and the community that he'd just driven through, get the sweat out of his armpits, he'd make a lot more sense talking to Kate and Kyle and Bryce and some of the other people he needed to speak with. It was funny how that happened, but often he wouldn't return calls until after he got clean. It was just his thing.

He dialed his wife.

"Hey, Kate, I'm here in my old room, but boy, do I

miss you."

She giggled. "Oliver and Kendall are taking a nap, so I'm going to whisper a little bit."

"That sounds kind of sexy."

"You think so? You're chicken to just turn around and come back."

"Well, that's what I want to talk to you about, Kate. I have to make this short because I need to make a few other calls too. But I wanted to let you know first that I got here. Also, I need to tell you this place looks like a war zone. I mean, I've seen villages in Nigeria that look better than that district where she had her gallery. Did you have any idea it was so dangerous here?"

"Not really. I mean, you know I don't dwell on the news. I just make it a point not to because I worry too much, especially if you're overseas. But it's hard to get the perspective, isn't it? You see it on TV, and yeah, it looks horrible, but you're sitting in your living room with your slippers and your flannel nightgown on, and somehow, it doesn't touch you. I can see it affected you. And I'm sorry it's worse than you thought."

"Well, I'm even more convinced than ever that they need to get out of here. They're being a little bit stubborn about it, but I just got here. There's a lot of moving parts. And I really need to speak with a fire inspector and their adjuster. Then I'll kind of get my bearings and be able to tell you how long it's going to take. I can't stay too long, because Kyle wants me back there. But holy crap, I had no idea that Mom and Dad were so vulnerable, and I think they're wrong about the arson."

"You don't think it was arson?" she asked.

"Oh, I think it was arson all right. But those warehouses that burned were not derelict buildings at all. They were some of the nicer buildings, the ones where people had come in and refurbished them, turned them into beautiful offices, galleries, studios. It sort of feels like somebody targeted some of the best buildings in the area and left the derelict buildings alone. It just doesn't feel right, Kate."

"I get it. Well, I trust your judgment, Tyler. You know better than anyone else in our family about that sort of thing, unfortunately. Am I allowed to share any of this with the other wives?"

Tyler was glad she asked permission. It was something they had forged together, this protocol.

"It'll be fine. I'm going to give Kyle a call now, so he'll be in the know. If this turns into a bigger project than I'm hoping it will, I may need some help from some of the guys, but I'm also going to talk to Colin Riley's old team and see if I can get a read on what's going on downtown. So just hang tight for a few days, maybe two or three at the most, and I'll update you as soon as I have things to tell you. Until then, don't worry."

"Said Tyler never."

She giggled, and it felt good to hear her laugh. Tyler couldn't find the space to return her laughter with some of his own.

Next, he called Kyle but had to leave a message.

"Hey, Kyle, it's Tyler. I just got to Portland. Mom and Dad are fine, but the studio is, well, it's leveled. And I have other concerns I'd like to talk to you about—not leave a message. So give me a call when you get a chance. I think two or three days is what I'm going to need, but one of the things I'm very clear on is that I've got to get my parents out of Portland. This area isn't safe for them any longer. And I have to tell you it reminds me of some of the war zones we've seen overseas. So give me a call back, and let's talk. But everything's fine, no changes in my ETA, and haven't spoken to the inspectors or the insurance people yet, but I need to bounce some things off you, and you're the first person who I think can help me with some advice. Take care. Kiss Christie for me, on the lips."

He smiled, figuring Kyle would get a kick out of that last comment. When he hung up the phone, he knew that his LPO would call him back within the hour unless he was in the middle of a briefing or a meeting of some kind.

Next person he called was his friend Bryce Tanner,

a former team guy and former San Diego police officer who had taken over the reins of Colin Riley's Bone Frog Protection Services, now owned by his daughter and daughter-in-law. Bryce had been on a hiring blitz ever since Mr. Riley's death a year ago.

"Hey, Tyler, boy, you're one of the guys I've got on my list to call this month. You interested in getting your separation orders?"

"No, not that. I don't know if you saw it in the news, but did you hear about the warehouse district fires that happened on Friday night?"

"Yeah?"

"Well, my mom's art gallery got burned to the ground. I came up here to help them. The fire investigator is saying it's arson. And I just frankly don't feel very comfortable with Mom and Dad rebuilding in that area or even being in Portland for that matter."

"Jesus Christ. You're fucking going to have to keep your damn mouth shut, Tyler. I've got several guys you used to work with on the team who are about ready to sign a contract with me. They hear you talking like that? They're going to back out. You can't do that to me."

"Well, if they have eyes in their head, they're going to see what I saw. It's an unstable situation. If we walked into a village like that, that's the first conclusion we'd come to. There's no welcome wagon here or people with flags—American flags greeting us or parades or anything like that. Everything looks normal until it all goes to hell, but there're little signs—the tag marks, the trash, the needles, and all the homeless, sort of an underground economy here. I'm just not at all happy with it, and I don't think anybody knows who's living here or what they're doing. It's just awful."

"I agree with you there. Part of that makes what we do a little more lucrative, but yeah, it's gotten pretty bad, I will admit that. Just don't go talking my new recruits out of it, okay, Tyler?"

"Deal. So I got to ask you, who do I need to talk to if I want the straight story on what's happening downtown and over at my mom's old warehouse?"

"Well, there are some really great cops still left in the city. We have a sheriff of a neighboring county that's probably better than the one who has jurisdiction here, but I think the police force and arson investigators on the fire department, they're probably your best guys. Most of them are real senior, and I think they pretty much can be trusted. We don't hold a very tight friendship on purpose, because we don't want to jeopardize their jobs, but I could get you a couple names if you want me to look into it."

"Hey, thanks, Bryce. I don't want to engage in conversation with the wrong person and then find out I started unraveling something I don't want to unravel. I want somebody to tell me the truth. I'm going to do that with the insurance company, but I need to figure out whether or not my parents were targeted in this arson or was their district targeted. And that's an important distinction. It means there's a different degree of safety that's required. I'm trying to figure out whether or not I need help."

"Well, Brother, we never served together on SEAL Team 3, but I got a lot of your buddies here, and we have a rule that we take care of our own. If you need us, you just give me a call, and I'll get some solid guys over. And we're not going to charge you either. I mean our business is good. Too good. You get my drift?"

"I do. So that explains why your offices are in Portland and not in, what?"

"Well, that's getting harder and harder to distinguish, isn't it, Tyler? I have to tell you that important people that have nice things are targets. I can't imagine your parents generating any kind of hatred or scorn against them, but just because of the fact that they are successful, took an old building, and turned it into a work of art, just like perhaps some of the other people there, makes them a target. I wouldn't worry too much about their safety. But I do think you're spot on about keeping them out of that neighborhood. If they were my parents? I wouldn't allow them to rebuild there. And I think things are going to change, but it might take a while."

"Well, my parents are getting up there in their seventies, so ten years won't make any difference to them. But thanks, Bryce, and I'll keep in touch. If you run across somebody you think I ought to talk to, you be sure to let me know. Text me if I don't pick up."

"You got it." He paused, and then added, "You knock up your wife again? You had two, I think it was, the last time?"

"Yeah, we got the two boys, eight and five, and now we have Kendall. She's nearly three."

"So Kate's got her little girl."

"Yes, sir. Otherwise, I'd be raising a small SEAL team. She's got her girl, and we're done."

"Well, good for you. I got two girls in college. I don't think I'm ever going to be able to retire now. After college comes weddings and maybe grandkids. I'm going to be working until I'm eighty years old, Tyler."

"Well, let's just hope things change before then. I got to go, Bryce, because I need to spend some time with the folks, but you take care and thanks for helping me out. I'll return the favor, Brother."

"Roger that, Tyler. Stay safe."

CHAPTER 7

KATE HAD A visit from her sister, Gretchen, who brought her youngest child, Angela, with her. Angela had been one of their go-to babysitters over the past year and was a very responsible fourteen-year-old. Her two older sisters were on their own, both in college.

"Mom gave me the news about Tyler's parents and the warehouse. God, Kate, that's horrible. Did they find out anything more?" Gretchen asked her.

Kate noted that her sister had great survival instincts, like a cat landing on all fours after a fall. She'd had some tough years, mostly raising her three daughters without much help from her first husband, a professional basketball player who broke just about every rule in parenting a dad could. She'd moved to Portland when they first got married to be near his team. Their very public divorce after Tony Sanders was caught on social media dancing and later dating several women outside his marriage, including a stripper, had been humiliating for Gretchen and the girls.

With Gretchen's oldest daughters in college, only Angela was still at home. When she started high school, Gretchen and Trace moved to Coronado, ending the commute and long patches away from the family between his deployments. It was challenging, but her sister adjusted first with the long-distance marriage and then the relocation and had even thrived under it all. Kate knew Trace was one of those rare breeds of man who became a father in every sense of the word to those three girls, who loved him dearly in return. He was madly in love with Gretchen and completely devoted to her happiness.

Gretchen was living her happily ever after, just like Kate was.

"I know he arrived safe this afternoon, and he's with his parents. I presume I'm going to hear some more tomorrow or maybe later on tonight. As of the time he called me, he hadn't met any of the fire inspectors or the insurance people yet. So his work is just starting."

Kate motioned to the living room couch and chairs, where they both sat. "You want anything?"

"I'm fine. Thanks." Gretchen was pensive then added, "I'm glad we moved out of Portland when we did. It had been such a great place for kids when they were growing up. Schools were good, and there were so many nice neighborhoods. They have a fantastic Children's Theater, youth symphony, lots of recreation department classes in dance, painting, and music. All that still exists, but now the whole downtown is just a mess. If we still lived there, I wouldn't allow the girls to take the bus like they used to before. Remember, we used to take the bus and go shopping? You came with us on a couple of occasions."

"I do. We could go everywhere by bus. It was very safe."

"Safe. That's what's missing now," Gretchen said, shaking her head. Kate noticed Angela was mum on the subject but looked as though she completely agreed.

"Tyler is going to try to convince them to move down here perhaps."

"I think that's an excellent idea. They must miss you guys and the grands. I don't know why they aren't camped at your doorstep twenty-four seven."

"His mom is so connected, and that gallery has been a great source of joy and inspiration for her. I don't think they ever would have considered leaving or rebuilding elsewhere if it hadn't been for the fire. We'll see. That's what he's helping them do, sort it out."

"They're lucky to have him. Glad he could get time off to do it." Glancing around the room, she noticed one of Mrs. Gray's bright paintings hanging over the fireplace mantle. "Is that one of hers?"

"It is. Beautiful, isn't it? So vibrant, alive. Makes you feel like you're standing in the middle of a tropical garden, doesn't it?" Kate said, admiring the huge painting.

Gretchen agreed. "So what else is new?"

"I have to tell you about this great class I took. It was an exploratory—all the different food, entertainment, and catering businesses that are available these days, everything from restaurants to onsite catering, even showed us a proforma about actually manning a gourmet food truck."

"A food truck? Wow."

"Yes. I'm really excited about it, enough to start looking into it. I've got more research to do, obviously, and Tyler hasn't completely signed off on it yet, as we haven't set up the logistics—you know how he is, planning things over and over again until it's perfect."

"God, Trace is the same way. All those guys are."

"We have to budget carefully, but it's either that or perhaps find a place down here where we could set up a wedding center, do sort of like what Devon and Nick are doing up in Santa Rosa."

"That sounds like fun. I could see you getting one of those vintage school buses and turning it into a lunch truck. Or maybe one of those old vegetable trucks. You remember those things you see occasionally? Mom used to love shopping there, remember?"

"Andy—the fruit produce guy, his name was Andy—used to come through the neighborhood, right?"

"That's right. And he used to flirt with all the housewives when their husbands were at work. But the vegetables were very fresh, and Mom swore by it."

They both laughed. Kate noted Angela rolled her eyes a bit.

"Anyway, there are a lot of things we used to do growing up that simply isn't around anymore, so as I was listening to the lecture about all these different options, I just fantasized on having this catering business and doing really healthy food truck choices, like healthy sandwiches, soups, juices, and some delicious keto, vegetarian, and gluten-free foods as well. I think people would pay a little bit more for good quality foods that help them with their diet or just for good health."

"I'm sold, Kate. I think you could do a great job. Yeah, an old vintage school bus, decorated shabby chic. Something really unusual with pretty curtains in it—maybe put in a table or two."

Kate shook her head. "There are certain health department things that are required, and I can't really have a restaurant on wheels, but I could set up tables outside and cater that way. I'm going to spend some time with Devon and Nick and really investigate all of that. Of course, first, we have to figure out what Tyler's parents are going to do. If we can get them down here and they can afford to buy, I think it's really the best solution."

"You're right, Sis. It's no place for them any longer. Too dangerous."

Kate wanted to include Angela in the conversation. "How's school, Angela?" she asked.

"Good. I made the varsity volleyball team, and I decided to quit basketball and just focus on volleyball. In the spring, I'm going to join a traveling team, so I get lots of exposure to college coaches."

"Good for you. Where do you want to go to school?"

"Well, San Diego State would be great, and they have a huge volleyball program. But I think anything on the West Coast here would be good for me. I'm not exactly sure what I'll be majoring in, getting my college paid for and playing volleyball are top of my list. I'll figure it out. Probably some kind of business or communications major."

"Well, if you're going to stay in the area and I do this food truck thing, maybe you can do some student research, come work for me part-time, maybe get school credit. I don't want to interfere with your team or family life, but we could sort of learn together, if you're up to it. I'll bet you'd whip your aunt pretty good in business. Probably teach me a few things," said Kate.

"What do you think of that, Angela?" Gretchen asked her.

She shrugged. "Sounds good. When are you going to start?"

"Oh, we're just making dreams, but maybe early next year if we can get the funds together to get the truck or buy the building. We're still looking at which way we want to go."

The two sisters caught up on other family business. Clover had met a nice boy from Colorado, and Gretchen expected there would be an announcement of an engagement coming soon.

"Is Trace going to walk her down the aisle? Or is Tony in good enough shape to do it?"

"No, Tony is out of their lives completely, even though he keeps trying to insert himself. I think Trace would be the one she'd ask, but it's up to her really. It's her wedding. And I'm probably putting the cart before the horse, so don't say anything to her if you happen to run across her. Also, Angela, don't tell your sisters I told your aunt this."

"Your secret is safe with me, Mom. Don't worry."

"And how's Rebecca doing? She's in junior college,

right?"

"Actually, she's working on her pilot's license. She was considering going into the Air Force, see if she could get some flying experience, but there's a good flight school, not the same as military training, but a pretty good flight school here, and she's already started taking classes. It's easier for a woman to get a pilot's license these days, so she's hoping she could start with one of the charter services and then work her way up to a large commercial airline. I've got a friend who's a triple seven pilot and loves it. Travels all over the world. Rebecca is all about travel and adventure."

"That sounds exciting. Good for her. I can see her being a pilot someday, although Rebecca and Clover are both over six feet. Don't they usually like pilots on the smaller side?"

"I don't think anything will stop her. Rebecca also coaches volleyball at the junior college to help pay for some of her fees. She's in an apartment now with four other girls, so Trace and I are almost empty nesters. Couple more years and Angela will be on her own somewhere. Not far away, we hope."

Kate smiled at the two of them. Gretchen had sworn off men completely until she met Trace on a celebratory vacation with several other SEALs and their wives and girlfriends. Tyler had introduced them. Gretchen had roomed with Linda Gray, Tyler's sister, who was a romance novelist. The two of them couldn't have been more different in personality.

"I'm glad things have worked out for you, and I'm also glad you moved down here. I imagine Trace is happier too."

Gretchen winced. "Well, he's actually considering getting out. You know he's forty-four, an old guy. I think this is going to be it."

"Tyler is thinking the same thing. Not quite having made the decision yet, but we're getting closer."

"Don't you have an enlistment coming up? It's always so tempting to take that bonus."

"It really is hard to turn down. But he feels like his body is giving out on him and one of these days he's going to hurt himself on a jump. His knees already cause a lot of pain, and he's going to probably have to have a new hip by the time he's fifty. So it takes a toll on him. I think he'd like to get out before he gets injured."

"So many of them retire on disability. It's just crazy how they survive. Tough guys."

"They are. They're the ones that get it done."

They heard some crying upstairs, and Kate recognized Kendall's voice.

"Uh-oh, I think we have a meltdown in process. I'll be right back—"

"I'll take care of it, Kate. Let me go see if I can

help," said Angela.

"Really? That's nice of you, thank you!" Kate sat back down as she watched Angela mount the stairs two at a time. "She's such a good girl, Gretchen. So responsible, and it'll be interesting to see what she winds up going into."

"They scatter all over, don't they? I've seen families posted to far regions of the world, and yet we all still stay so close. Even the kids like to stay together. I think it's from years of bonfires and backyard picnics and team gatherings."

"I know the other teams are not exactly like Team 3. Trace and Tyler are lucky," added Kate.

"Tell me about it. Trace came from Team 8. He's never regretted that decision. That's why, when we first got together, he didn't mind the commuting. He had three girls to get to know, and he wanted to be home on the weekends. We made it work. He's the dedicated father that they should have had from the get-go."

"You're all lucky to have him be part of your lives. I'm so happy for you. You look healthy, excited. I've never seen you happier, Gretchen."

She gave Kate a quick smile before it disappeared. She began slowly. "So... if Trace gets out, he's looking at that security company several of the members of the police force and other teams, special ops guys have been joining lately. He told me Tyler also thinks very highly of the group."

"Yeah, he's setting up for an interview when they get back from the next deployment. I guess it's Mexico again." Kate said.

"That's what I understand too. God help us."

Kate hesitated to ask but knew that Tyler would be asking himself if he were there.

"Gretchen, Tyler may need some help up in Portland. He doesn't know for sure but he did tell me that he's planning on only being there two or three days. If it gets more involved or if he needs some help, he might be reaching out to several guys that are either from the area or familiar with Portland proper. I just wanted to give you a heads-up. You might mention it to Trace."

"Will do. I know he'd help any way he can. I'm so sorry about that warehouse and all those lovely things ruined. Your mother-in-law is one of the nicest ladies I've ever met. The first artist I've met who really wasn't weird, you know what I mean?"

"I agree. Our mom calls herself a hippie all the time, but Tyler's mom, she still is. She's the real deal."

The two had a good laugh together, then embraced, called upstairs to Angela who brought Kendall downstairs in her arms.

"Here you go honey, here's your mom." Angela handed the three-year-old over to her mother.

"What was it all about?" Kate asked Angela.

"I think Oliver pushed her off the bed. He didn't want to come downstairs because I think he suspects you're mad at him."

"Well, thanks for the heads-up. You think you'd be available this weekend to babysit? I'm hoping Tyler will be home and we talked about going to a game."

"Yeah, I'm free. Just let me know. Send me a text."

"Okay, Kate, you take care and please update me if you hear any news. You want me to set up some meal deliveries or something like that?" Gretchen asked.

"Oh, no, this isn't that type of a thing. And besides I'm home and able to care for the kids." She checked her watch. "Oh my gosh, I've got to go get Grady at school."

"Give our love to Tyler. We'll be praying for Deidre and Larry. And you too, Sis. Please let us know if we can help in any way."

Kate called for Oliver to come downstairs. She quickly strapped them both into car seats in the Suburban. On the way to the pickup, she thought to herself how lucky she was to be able to live in a beautiful place like San Diego, with a loving husband who was actually considering joining her in business. It put an extra bounce in her step, the thought of all the new possibilities, giving her energy, and a lightness of being she hadn't felt for several years.

Change isn't always bad. It depends on how you manage it, she thought to herself.

Of course, being married to the right man, a true and loving partner, didn't hurt either.

CHAPTER 8

"HEY, TYLER, HOW'S it going?" Kyle was returning his call.

"Really nothing to report, except I'm looking for solid guys that I can talk to. Kyle, you wouldn't believe what that place looks like. I don't think there's anything standing more than about two or three feet tall. It's just smoke and ash charcoal. It's awful. And it affected a whole string of buildings going down several blocks. What a mess."

"How are they holding up?"

"Pretty good. I think they're still in shock."

"I'll bet. I know I would be, that's got to be a tough one. But at least nobody's hurt."

"Yeah that's what I told them too. The part that kind of gets to me and this is what I wanted to talk to you about Kyle, my folks are incredibly naive. I mean, you know they traveled all over during their hippie days in the sixties and seventies. They had a good time and they're used to being and talking to a lot of people—being free spirits, you know?"

"I got you. They've had a good life. They've seen it all."

"Yes. And they've always been great supporters of causes, they've helped the poor and they've worked with different groups. They're very socially responsible people. That's kind of why this whole thing bothers me, because I mean, my parents are the good guys. They're the guys with the white hats. It just is so unfair that they would be the ones who would get the brunt of all of this. Understand?"

"Since when is the world fair? Tyler, you've seen some shit overseas, there's just no rhyme or reason to it. Even when we think there is we go over there and you know, it's just a mess. Sometimes I think we're just glorified policemen, keeping people from blowing each other up, but I don't know if we really solve anything."

"True. You're right there."

"Your parents are just dealing with the world in a different way. I mean no offense Tyler, but we don't want people like your folks running things right? We don't want to have to go to them for our protection. That's why they got guys like us."

"Yeah, I agree with that a hundred percent. And I guess if it was just a random attack, I wouldn't feel this way. But I have a gut feeling that it's not. I have the feeling that they were targeted and it's just, you know when we get those hunches?"

"Hunches keep us alive sometimes Tyler. I say listen to them. But logically, why do you think they would be targeted?"

"It was something that the fire marshal told my dad the first day. He thinks that it started at their building, and then went on down the blocks from there. And all the buildings that were targeted were the ones that had been recently renovated, fixed up. So if this was some kind of a protest against economic opportunity or protesting some kind of inequity of some kind, why would they target the buildings that were improving the neighborhood?"

"Well, think about it Tyler. All these people coming in and fixing up the area, makes it less affordable for other people. Who knows, maybe somebody has an ax to grind on that score."

"Well, I didn't think about that actually. But it does make some sense."

"So are they going to be okay with the rebuild? Are they going to get reimbursed for what her art is really worth?" Kyle asked him.

"I've read the policy. Boy, talk about putting you to sleep. It's worse than reading a dictionary. The way they've got all the fine print everywhere. And right on the top of the policy it says this is in plain English, easy to read. I say bullshit."

Kyle chuckled. "Welcome to the world of owning real estate."

"So do we have orders yet or timing set up?"

"We do. It's going to be sooner than we thought. I'm thinking the middle of next month. They're trying to coordinate some treasury department things first before they go after this particular cartel. They don't want to send us down there unless they've got all their ducks in a line. I was meeting with the head shed today as a matter of fact. We'll take a tight group, not a big team at all. You can put in for a skip over if you want, but if you're going to re-up, you could do it in Mexico. And I didn't say that."

It was Tyler's turn to chuckle. "I haven't gotten there yet Kyle. I just am not prepared to make a decision. You know that Kate has been kind of on me to consider doing something else. She's got her heart set on getting involved in a business like catering or running a food truck."

"A food truck? Why the fuck would you want to do that? You mean like spreading mayonnaise all over white bread and shit like that? You think that would be fun compared to what you've been doing the last ten years?"

Tyler had to admit Kyle had a point there. That was the one part he hadn't considered, since it would be hard to find excitement in operating a food truck. He'd considered it because Kate was so over the moon about it.

"I keep telling myself, and I guess it's really repeating what Kate has to say, that I need to do something that's less dangerous. But doing dangerous is what I do."

"Doing dangerous is what you do well, Tyler. And I got to tell you, I would miss you a ton. So don't be thinking about that too lightly. I mean if she wants to go do the catering and stuff let her do it. But man, standing in a hot kitchen or a little cramped food truck space inhaling all that gas, wearing a dirty apron and having your face and fingers all greasy, just doesn't sound like any kind of fun I'd like to do. I'd rather go get a $5 an hour job at the YMCA and lifeguard rather than do that."

"Yeah. You're right. I knew it was the right thing to call you."

"God damn it Tyler. Did I just talk you out of becoming a professional chef?"

"Well, I think you might have. Anyway I will give you a call before I come back. So far I don't see anything that's going to take me any longer. But you never know. I'm going to try to wrap it up tomorrow if I can."

"That sounds good to me we'd love to get you back

home. You take care now. Give my love to Kate when you talk to her."

"Roger that Kyle."

TYLER WAS STILL thinking about Kyle's words long after he'd showered, and tried to lay down for a short nap before dinner. He finally just got up, got dressed, and went downstairs to help his mom prepare.

"You get all your phone calls in?" his mom asked.

"Yes, I did. Had to leave a message for Kate, but she'll call me back later. How are you doing?" He placed his arm around her shoulder and pulled her to him.

"I think I'm going to be fine, Tyler. You know, it just is what it is. Oh, and your dad has the adjuster coming over tomorrow. I think he's sent Dad a list of things, a piece of paper he needs to fill out for the claim. Maybe you could help him with that after dinner."

"Happy to. So does he sound like a pretty reasonable guy then?"

"I have no idea. I'm beginning to think I've been living in an alternate reality. I get so involved in my paintings—all the color, form, and structure—it's like I'm in my own world. I think this whole situation has actually been beneficial for me."

Tyler leaned back against the kitchen countertop

and examined his mother cocking his head to the side. "Mother, I never thought I'd hear you say that." When she looked up from her food prep, he gave her a huge smile. "I think you may be right. Sometimes change is good."

She blushed. "The good news is, your dad keeps pretty good records. He never throws anything out, so it's just a matter of going through things. That's what he's doing now in the study. But I think we'll be able to justify all of those pictures. The good news is we had them all photographed for the color catalog we were going to be making. That was just a stroke of genius. And Tyler, I've been thinking a lot about what you told us this afternoon at the warehouse. I probably have been awfully naive when it comes to spending a lot of time down there, especially at night. I guess I should be thankful that it's just a fire that destroyed the building, when it could have been much worse. But in my mind, I'd like to see the world a perfect place, where these things don't happen, where people treat each other respectfully. But that just isn't the case is it?"

"You've got that right, Mom. That's why they have to have guys like us. It's hard for people to understand the need for real protection. People only take it lightly until they get affected themselves."

"Well, I certainly have a newer appreciation for what you've had to go through. And I love that you call yourself a force for good. That's just brilliant." She followed it up with a warm smile.

Tyler's dad entered the kitchen. "So this is where it's all happening right?"

"Nah, I'm just kind of distracting her a little bit. I'm really not much help."

"I thought you were going to go into the catering business with your wife?"

Tyler was quiet for a second, realizing he wasn't really very good in the kitchen, in fact, he was horrible unless it was serving a beer or barbecuing hamburgers or a steak. Kate had done all the cooking, knew everything there was to know about wines, and was a real foodie. Tyler never acquired that.

"I kind of like the idea of spending a lot more time around Kate. I'm not so sure I'm going to be much help, but we'll see. We're still talking. Nothing's set in stone yet. First thing in our order of business is to figure out what's going on with you guys up here. And then we've got lots of time for the rest of it."

"Well, I put together a list for the adjuster. He's coming tomorrow, by the way."

"Mom told me."

"I have all the receipts for the remodeling, and I have the escrow papers from when we bought the building back 15 years ago, I even have a full rundown of all the expenses outside of the remodeling. I couldn't believe how much money we spent on permits and fees, inspections, engineering. We had to make sure the structure was sound in order to allow events in the building where people would come and food would be served. We worked our asses off."

"There's always one person in the family that has to be good with the records. For us it's Kate, I admire you, Dad. The more records you have, I think the better this will be for you."

They spent the evening eating slowly, talking about what it was like to grow up in Portland, all the memories they had raising the family. They even talked about Tyler's first school dates, and the time Linda's prom date backed out so she took her best friend, a girl. Caused all kinds of ruckus in the school. They talked about some of the camping trips they'd been on, and the first time Tyler had seen a butterfly when he was a toddler.

"You were such a beautiful boy, people kept asking me if you were a girl. Those blue eyes, and your curly hair, I have to admit I let it get a little bit too long. But by the time you made it to kindergarten, Tyler, you were all boy, active, running around. I remember being called into the teacher's office when you were in second grade, she told me that you were hyperactive. She mentioned that she thought you should be evaluated to take medication to calm you down. I knew that that would ruin your spirit. I knew that would be a huge mistake. I wouldn't let them test you."

"You should have, Mom. Who knows what they would've found?"

They all had a chuckle over that one. His mother added, "No I think you were intended to be exactly how you are, right in the middle of everything, saving the day and showing everybody else how to be strong. I can't tell you how wonderful it is to have you help us Tyler, to have you come up here and give of yourself, just spend some time with us. I guess what happens when you get old is you start becoming the child and your kids start being the adult. I used to think I wouldn't like that, but it's rather pleasant. I like seeing you in this leadership role. And with this family, that's going to happen more and more."

"Mom, that's very astute. I'm not offended by that comment, and that's why it encourages me because, and I know I've said it before, probably more than four or five times now, I really want you to consider not rebuilding on that site. And as a plan B to that, I really want you to consider moving down to San Diego with us. All the things that you do here you can do there. The difference will be I can watch out for you guys, you've got your grandkids to spend time with and Kate, and the weather's better. I won't worry so much when I'm overseas. There's a lot of really good reasons for you to do that. But I won't force you into doing anything."

His mother was always emotionally more astute than his father, Tyler thought. He was satisfied that things were going in the right direction just by hearing her comment.

He went to bed satisfied, and was able to fall asleep immediately.

Of course, that's when Kate called back.

"Tyler? Is that you?"

Tyler realized he had answered the phone and it was placed to his ear, but whatever he'd said to her didn't make any sense whatsoever. "I think you just heard part of my dream. I think I was dreaming in Ferengi?"

"That's funny. That's really funny, Tyler. So how is everything today?"

"Well, we're seeing the adjuster tomorrow morning. He's coming to the house, and I think I'm going to head back home maybe tomorrow or the next day. I need to touch base with the inspector, but you know, Mom and Dad are actually coming around to the idea of maybe moving to San Diego. Maybe Mom could help you in your business, Kate."

"Oh, that's not necessary. I'm going to have a big strong former Navy SEAL to help me. Besides, I think just having you in the lunch wagon or with me at catered events is going to be good for business. I'm going to show off those tats, those shoulders, and I'm going to let you bat your big baby blue eyes all you like."

He wanted to laugh at the comment, but he found it a little offensive. Was it all coming down to that? He was some kind of Adonis who would be paraded through town? He hoped she was just being lighthearted and making fun of the situation. But he wasn't really sure he wanted to do something he wouldn't be very good at. That bothered him. So did that make him a monster then?

"Tyler? Are you okay?"

"Sorry. I had tried to take a nap this afternoon, and I was just wired, couldn't do it. And I fell asleep tonight, and it just felt like I went into a coma. And then you called. I'm just not thinking straight."

"Well, you call me tomorrow. I won't keep you, and I've got a sitter lined up in case you want to go to the baseball game on Saturday. I have someone that'll give us a couple of tickets. Do you think you'd want to do that?"

"Sure. Are we taking the kids?"

"No, that's who the sitter is for. I figured just you and I go do something fun."

"That's probably a good idea. Kyle told me today that we may be leaving the middle of next month.

They've bumped everybody up over a month."

"Oh, that's too bad. I was hoping we'd have a decent summer."

"Well, it is what it is, I guess we don't want to go down there unless they're ready for us, right?"

"That's true. So when will you know for sure?"

"I think it's for sure already. We'll know the exact date probably in a week or two. So I've got to sign off here, but before I do, just want to let you know I love you, and I think we'll make this work somehow with my folks. I really do think I can convince them."

"I think the kids would be ecstatic. Maybe this fire was a good thing, Tyler. It gives us all a chance to look at the future. I talked to Gretchen today, she came over."

"Oh really?"

"She said that Trace is considering joining that group up in Portland. And she told me that you were interested in it too. Is that true?"

Tyler wondered where they had gotten that impression. He did have favorable feelings about the group. He knew that Bryce was running a tight ship, and he knew it was a pleasant alternative to staying in the military, and he'd probably make a lot more money. He hadn't quite resolved the situation of living in Portland, however. That was a non-starter to him, especially now.

"I really didn't give Trace or anybody a positive read on doing that. And I don't want to live in Portland, Kate. Especially now. Trace, well, it's different for him, you know Gretchen spent a lot of time there and the kids are familiar with it. It might make sense for him, but honestly we haven't talked that much about it. Just a little. No, I'm happy where I'm at."

"Except you're going to be leaving the Teams, right?"

Little bells and whistles were going off in the back of Tyler's head. She wanted an answer in the affirmative. He wasn't going to be able to give her that. He inhaled deeply and decided to just suck it up and tell her what was going on with him.

"I've just got to be sure, Kate. I've got to be sure whatever it is I do next, if I leave the Teams, that I've got enough in my tank, that I stay the same man I am now as a SEAL. I don't want to lose that. My goal isn't to be Tyler Gray light. My goal is to be super awesome protector of the world Tyler Gray. As long as whatever I do after I leave the Teams, as long as I can still say that, I'll be happy. Until then, well, we're just going to have to let time reveal itself to us, okay Kate?"

"It wasn't what I wanted to hear, but I do understand. It's hard doing this on the phone. We'll talk about it when I can see you face to face. I think I understand what you're saying, and I don't want Tyler light either. But I was hoping that you would give me a chance to show you what I can do. I really want to try to do something, have my own business, have our own business. It's important to me. But if it's not something you want to do, you're right. You shouldn't. And I think we'll know in time. So waiting to have that discussion later, that's okay."

"Thank you Kate. I love you more every day. Thank you for always supporting me. I'm going to do whatever I can to try to return the favor."

"You already have, Sweetheart. But I don't mind you trying even more."

CHAPTER 9

T HE INSURANCE ADJUSTER arrived at Tyler's parents' home at 9:00 a.m., sharp. He was younger than Tyler expected, appearing to be barely 30 years old. Tyler showed him to a place on the couch, and kept up a light banter until he started honing in on the man's experience.

"Wait a minute, I know you are their son, but this is really between my insurance company and your parents, Tyler. So if you don't mind, I'd like to ask them some questions and go over their paperwork and then we can have a little chat afterwards if you like. But I don't have to take up a lot of your time if we can just do it that way, please."

Tyler consented.

Mr. Gray showed the adjuster all the information he'd gathered on the pictures, as well as sharing with him the folder with all the fix-up receipts he'd collected during the 15 years they'd owned the building. They had renovated it twice, once to make it habitable, installing air conditioning and an adequate heating system. The second installation was to finish off the walls and install the beautiful hardwood flooring. He also demonstrated to the adjuster his tax base, reflective of the fact that they did all the work with permits, as required, and hired a contractor to do so. Except for some painting and sanding, none of the work was done themselves, but was organized and run by them.

"Well, you've just made my job much easier. We have you insured for a million dollars for the building, which may be more than the replacement cost, but as far as retail value it's probably underinsured for value. So, if you can accept the value at a million as a payoff, we can perhaps build in some other things to get you more money in other categories. You have policy limits for relocating your business, and also policy limits for medical expenses if someone had been harmed in the fire. We don't have to use those funds, so we may be able to earmark some of that unused portion for something that you really need so that we can get you the accurate amount."

Tyler was impressed with the way he ran the meeting.

"You're actually going to help them get what they think is fair, is that correct? There's no right or wrong way to do this, it's just you're going to try to get from the insurance company what my folks are asking or needing to get. Is that right?"

"That's right, I'm a private adjuster, not an insurance representative. We do it differently here and we think it's better for the homeowner. Technically I work for your parents not the insurance company, even though they assign me and pay my fees. But I do know how the insurance company works, and I'm like the go-between between them and the customer. If we can come to terms quickly, then we don't have to get involved in any other preliminary rulings or decisions. We can just move forward. It's kind of a new approach to handling claims and losses. We really have a hard time doing it when it involves somebody who has died or there's been a major accident with the claim. Those can be quite expensive because there's wrongful death, other liabilities and court proceedings that can occur, and can delay the claim payout greatly. But in this case, since we're just talking about replacement value of a building and property of a certain value, it should be fairly simple."

"How soon before we get the proceeds?" asked Tyler's mom.

"It depends on what we agree to. It's my job to negotiate that for you. You could sell the lot at a salvage value, be paid for the loss of the building and not rebuild it, take the money and do something else with it, or you could get some plans drawn and build the building all over again, which may take a while because you need to have permits, you need to hire an architect, engineers, all that sort of thing and it can take months, sometimes even a year to get started on that. It really depends on what your future plans are. If you need this building and you want this location, then that would be the route you would take. If you don't, my recommendation is going to be take the money and then use it elsewhere."

Tyler still had questions about the findings of the fire report.

"So what if they find out this was intentionally set?" Tyler asked him.

"That only complicates things if there's some kind of suspicion that your parents or someone they hired torched the building. I'm not hearing that at all, and frankly I'd be surprised if they were blamed for it. We all know what's been going on downtown. Our insurance company is in fact re-evaluating carrying insurance in Portland, so we may be looking for ways to disassociate ourselves. That might mean settling quickly. That's a good thing for your folks."

"So, you'll leave this market then?"

"We may not be writing new policies. Not every insurance company can insure against demonstrations and protests, riots, we're not supposed to discriminate on the basis of that, however, if losses and claims are high in a particular city, it's very common for an insurance company to roll back their new policy goals."

Satisfied, they'd received everything they needed, the adjuster told him he would take the copies Mr. Gray had given him and would write up a report that he wanted them to approve before he submitted it.

"After it's submitted, we have approximately 14 days for the company to answer, they will do so in writing, and if what they propose is acceptable to you then based on what you choose, we'll go forward."

After the gentleman left, Tyler felt extremely positive about the meeting. "Good job, Dad. You nailed it." Tyler said.

His father shrugged. "I'm one of these people that if I don't have the paperwork filed properly in the right files, I can't sleep at night. I never thought it would be useful in this kind of situation. But I get great peace of mind out of being organized, Tyler. Believe it or not."

Tyler's parents received word that they could meet with the fire inspectors down at the property later in the day. The three of them took the VW bus again, parking it several blocks away to keep from picking up debris, glass, and nails, and walked the distance to the site of the old building.

Several fire officials were having a small conclave in front of the former structure. One of the gentlemen stepped forward extending his hand to Mr. and Mrs. Gray.

"I'm Craig Moorehead. I'm in charge of the investigation, sort of the liaison between our department and the city. How do you do?" He shook both of their hands. And then he addressed Tyler. "I understand you're still serving in the armed forces?"

"Yes sir, I'm in the Navy sir."

"God bless you son, and I thank you for your sacrifice."

Tyler noticed Mr. Moorehead was a no-nonsense type of guy, probably with some military training, and got right to the point.

"We believe that this particular incident started very close to the stroke of midnight. You will see we found evidence that an accelerant had been used, and it appeared to have started in this corner of the building, with additional accelerants added all along the far wall that came up close to the dead shrubbery for the adjacent property. I can't walk you in to show you, but I can give you pictures, if you like."

"No, that's not necessary," said Tyler's mom.

"Okay good. This shrubbery probably ignited right away, and we had the fire traveling down the street. This person or persons who did this is very familiar with setting fires, probably has been trained, and while we don't know what they used as an accelerant, we believe it's a derivative of gasoline of some kind, possibly a thick pasty mixture, that could be painted on the side of a building and ignited. It's very expensive to use. It's used in fire control for controlled burns, and in some military operations, but it's a derivative of the gasoline refining process, and is actually something that we dispose of."

"Who would have access to this?" Tyler asked.

"Other than the folks who transport it to superfund dump sites, someone who has worked in forestry, or the military. But most of this product is disposed of, not used."

"That leaves it kind of open, then," he said.

"Perhaps. Only certain people are licensed to handle this type of material, so it narrows down who the suspects could be. However, I'm going to guess that we're going to find some site or manufacturing plant that has reported recent theft of this material. It's very sophisticated, and this is not created by a homeless person or someone who was looking to break in and use the building for shelter. That's going to rule out 99% of the people who live here."

"So what you're saying is it's someone from the outside?" Tyler asked.

"Yes sir, I am saying that."

Tyler and his parents shared expressions of wonder and disgust between the three of them, and then Tyler added more questions.

"So, it appears that this could have been created by somebody who was protesting downtown? Is that what you're saying, that there's a link between the two?"

"I am. We found some of this accelerant painted on several automobiles, used to fully engulf a car and cause an explosion. It works quite well with that. We also have some surveillance video that shows someone with a paintbrush and a paint can painting some pasty liquid on places that were later ignited. So we're fairly sure we're talking about one individual since that's all we've got on surveillance footage and he's obviously a trained professional fire starter. That's not a technical term folks, it's just how we say it, fire starter."

"So this was done after the demonstration downtown, which I understand was kind of completed by 11 o'clock or so? Is that right?" Tyler asked.

"There were still some loiterers and people that were being watched, but yes more or less everything was over by 11:00. I would say they knew that they were going to come over here and although it doesn't appear we had huge crowds, just a handful of people here, I would say they had it all planned that way. This was not a protest. This was pure destruction of property."

"Man, I didn't realize you could figure all that out from the evidence. That's amazing." Tyler said.

"Well, sir, I'm just giving this to you verbally because you are the property owners and because of your service, Mr. Gray. I always treat my military families like they should be, like they deserve. However, our investigation is still ongoing, and by the time I issue the final report, many things could have changed. So please don't quote me, please don't give this information to anyone outside of this little group here, and I will make sure to keep you informed as to how we're investigating, and ultimately, hopefully when we catch someone. I'm going to tell you right now, after working several of these types of incidences up in the Seattle area, which was my job before I came to Portland, I would be surprised if this particular person who did this is still in the state of Oregon. They're probably long gone."

"So do you call in the feds then?" Tyler wondered.

"Already done. They have an extensive lab, a lot more resources than we have here in Portland, so that will be the next step. And we also haven't finished our surveillance search. Not much in the way of camera footage here in this neighborhood but of course downtown, there's lots of footage. With facial recognition software, and you didn't hear that from me, we feel fairly certain we'll find the person or persons who are responsible for this. I just want to reassure you."

"You think that the fire started at their building

and then moved down. Do you have any idea why they chose my parents' building?"

"Yes and no. I think it was targeted because it was one of the nicest buildings down here. I think it was not intended to cause body count loss, done carefully in such a way that it wouldn't cause any loss of life. They did it at midnight. This area has no surveillance cameras set up, and possibly they had scoped out the site ahead of time and determined that. They may have even been inside the building itself. I think it's a combination of all those. Opportunity, making a statement, getting the biggest bang for the buck so to speak."

"So do you think it's possible this is *personal* against them?"

"No I don't. I really don't. I think they were unlucky enough to have done a good job remodeling the building. That in and of itself made them a target."

CHAPTER 10

KATE WAS DELIGHTED when she got the call from Tyler that he was coming home early. He had missed the flight for today, but was scheduled to be out tomorrow, and would be arriving home in the middle of the afternoon. She spent the day cleaning the house, changing the sheets on the bed and getting her nails done. It had been several months since she'd indulged in such delicacies, and without the help of Angela, providing babysitter services for Kendall, she would not have been able to do it. She came home with sparkly red polish which she hoped her returning hunk of a husband would thoroughly enjoy.

She purchased a couple of Tyler's favorite steaks, bone-in rib eye and had spaghetti fixings out so the kids could have their special food as well. She rented a movie for them, and washed her hair, shaved her legs and did everything she could after the cleaning and cooking, to make sure she was more than presentable.

Gretchen had asked if she could help, but Kate wanted to work on the house by herself, listening to all her favorite music, singing to the songs, and even managing to get a little bit of gardening time in to refresh the flowers in her front yard.

She got the kids to retire early and set herself up in the bedroom, reading one of her new books.

She'd been concerned about Tyler's comment about perhaps revisiting the idea of leaving the teams. Her hope was that she could convince him that leaving and joining a partnership with her, would be something not only better suited for their family, less dangerous too, but something he would actually enjoy. She knew he loved his job as a Navy SEAL, but she also knew he was concerned about his physical capabilities and didn't want to retire on a disability.

She reviewed some online courses on the catering business, and even explored several resources for purchasing either used food trucks, or brand-new retrofits. The brand-new vehicles were going to be out of her price range, but there were a decent number of trucks that had come on the market recently, due to the pandemic, and she flagged a couple of them to show Tyler when he got home. It was all doable with the money they had saved, and if they got a small home equity loan, that would be all they would need to finish equipping not only her home but perhaps renting a kitchen space downtown. She even talked to a commercial Realtor about doing so and he was on the lookout for such an opportunity.

She got a call from Christy just after the kids went down to sleep.

"So Tyler's coming back. I was going to call you and just say if you needed to have coffee or get together, I'm available. But now that he's coming home, I guess I was a little bit too late," Christy said.

"You've got so many other things to do, Christy, I'm good, but boy, I'm so impressed by how much you do for us. Thank you for thinking of me, but please don't waste your time here. I'd love to have coffee with you, but I know you're busy and you have your career as well."

"Well, it can be done you know."

That's when Kate suspected that Kyle might have put Christy up to the phone call.

"Yeah, I understand. I don't know that I could do it like you do though, since you've got your husband to take over the kids on a regular basis, I don't see how he does that either, but I don't know if I could concentrate doing real estate, and then also managing the kids. I mean I guess I should ask you how you do it?"

"Well, you get used to it. Remember when I first got together with Kyle, I was a successful Realtor or trying to be, and I had it in me to make it go long before we had kids. I think that with your experience in the wine industry, and what you know about customer service and catering at the wineries, you would be a good fit. So you actually have worked in the field you want to pursue. As far as Tyler being part of it, I'm just not sure about that. You're going to have to wait and see."

Kate noticed she didn't accuse her of trying to get Tyler off the teams, but she also didn't want to appear to be confrontational or against the move. It was very smart of her, and if Kyle coached her, he did a good job.

"Well, I realize this would be all on me. Part of me thinks I should try to get it up and running first and then bring Tyler in. But the other part of me realizes that I need help. And I can't do it by myself. Unlike you selling real estate I don't think I could do this just myself."

"I know you've thought about this, Kate, but maybe there are others out there that could give you a hand. However, one thing you're going to have to look at: he's a man of action. And sometimes these things don't work out the way we expect them to. I mean Kyle, I will tell you, is not the best person to babysit the kids but we do it to save money. And it forces him to spend more time there. Otherwise, he'd be down at the gym, he'd be talking to the guys, he'd be exploring ways he could run his team better. And I have to pull him back and make him do things that bring him into the family, even though I know he loves us all, I have to force him to stay involved."

"Like I said, I'm in awe. You actually have to remind him to stay involved?"

"And he knows that, so he puts up with it. But boy, there are some days I come home and Kyle is just a total basket case. Those kids have driven him up the wall and down the other side. And they know it too. He's a pushover. Not with the team, but with his kids. So we'll see."

"I never thought about that. Tyler has told me some stories, though."

Christy laughed. "Oh yes, we have the stories. You remember the one when we found Gunny's ashes delivered to the house with the lost luggage?"

"A classic tale. I've heard the story from both of you. Hilarious!"

"Truth is, the kids will eventually leave our home, at least the first two in just a couple of years, and he's going to have to face his future without them. I don't think he's going to make a good Realtor though. I would never make him do that."

Kate could see what kind of a salesman Kyle would make. She giggled.

"I think that's funny, Christy. And thank you for

sharing that. By the way, I wanted to ask you about commercial spaces. I've been talking to another broker who had a sign in a little off-street that I thought would be perfect for renting a kitchen. Do you ever run across those?"

"Not often. I'm mostly specialized in residential sales. But I'd be happy to get one of our commercial guys to give you a call and maybe show you around if you want."

"Well, let me first talk to Tyler and maybe he has some thoughts. I don't want to waste anybody's time. There's also the possibility that something may be happening with his parents moving down here. I mean we can only hope and dream, right?"

"I loved my mother to death, I really did. I never knew my father. But I loved my mother with all my heart. She wanted me to come down to San Diego long before she passed, and I just, I wanted to make it on my own, you know what I mean?"

"I know exactly what you mean, Christy."

"But I think if we had lived together, honestly, it wouldn't have worked. She needed her space, and I needed mine. And yes, we loved each other, we were so close, but sometimes you can be too close. And I think that's the way it would have been. Life has a way of working itself out and honestly, Kate, I don't have the answers, but if you just keep your eyes open, the right opportunity is bound to happen. I don't think we should force it. At least that's my philosophy."

"Wow—"

"Okay, and I'm sorry. Lecture over," said Christy.

"I didn't take it that way, but you gave me a lot of things to think about, and I promise you I will take it to heart."

"I understand Angela's been babysitting for you. Is she good and is she available like for other SEAL families?" Christy asked.

"I think so. Up to her of course. She doesn't drive so you have to pick her up or have Gretchen drop her off, but she's very responsible and the kids love her. She likes to read to them and do coloring projects and things. I haven't had her take the kids outside of the house because, well, she doesn't drive. So I haven't tried that but for just straight babysitting at home, I think she's ideal. And I don't like the idea of hiring older kids even though I know several SEAL kids that would be fine. I just think she's the perfect age and the right temperament to do what she does. And I think she appreciates the extra money."

"Boy, that's good enough for me. I've had some inquiries, and I don't want to allow Brandon to babysit. It's just a whole different thing with having your son babysit other people's kids. Kyle and I have been against it. There's lots of other things he can do to earn money anyway. But I will certainly pass her name and Gretchen's phone number around with that recommendation and maybe you'll get some calls for references. Thank you, Kate."

"Happy to recommend her. Okay, well, I'm going to turn in early. I've got a few errands to run tomorrow morning early before I pick him up."

THE NEXT MORNING, Kate kept Kendall in the Suburban after dropping Oliver and Brady off at school. She drove to the store picking up a few last-minute items she'd forgotten to do the day before, took them home and then headed to the airport. She got a text from Tyler saying that the plane had actually arrived early, so he was already waiting at the pick-up station when she drove up.

Putting the car in park, she burst open the driver door and ran to his arms.

"God, Kate. I think I'll go away more often if this is what I come home to," he said as he kissed her.

She was pleased that he gave her the response she was hoping for.

"That wouldn't make a bit of difference, but it's wonderful to see you again and I'm glad it didn't take longer. Everything okay up there?"

"As good as it can be. We're still a wait and see."

They heard some honking and the traffic control

officer was asking them to move along. Tyler threw his duty bag in the second seat, kissed Kendall who was screaming with her arms outstretched to hug her daddy, and then took over the driver duties as Kate slid over. He started the Suburban and carefully maneuvered them onto the freeway.

"I've got to pick up Oliver, and do you suppose we could do that on the way home?" she asked.

"Of course. I'm all yours."

"So will you have to go back up there soon or is this it for now?" she asked.

"I don't know. A lot of it depends on what they find, and if the adjuster comes in with a number that Mom and Dad can live with. They stand to walk away with quite a chunk. But they're going to have to decide where they want to live and what they want to do. And, you know how I've tried to encourage them, but I just have to let them make up their own mind."

"Of course you do. I'm so glad you were there though to give them a hand."

"You know I was kind of wary of what kind of support we were going to get up there, but the police and fire, the detectives that I've spoken to, they're all pretty darn good. And I talked to the Bone Frog Group, Bryce, who you remember right?"

"Oh the former SEAL and who became a policeman?"

"Yep, that's him. He said that the senior members of the police and fire departments up there are very qualified, very good, and he said that many of them are pushing to retire early, due to all the turmoil there. But for right now, we've got really good people on the case."

"So have they determined why their place was burned, I mean was it part of the protest then?"

"We still don't know. They are looking for suspects. Once that happens, then we'll probably know further but it's just a guess at this point. It doesn't really matter one way or the other except that they'll get their money, and I think it will affect where they invest it. And that's kind of the way it's going to be for them."

"I see. They wouldn't want to go back to an area where they had problems, is that what you're saying?"

"Exactly."

"How did it look?"

"You know I had déjà vu in my old room, and you remember when Grady was learning to play soccer and we came up for that tournament?"

"Yes, he was so excited. His first road trip with his dad."

"While I was laying there in bed looking at all my trophies and I thought about what it was like growing up there. I really have a lot of happy memories. I hope they can get it together to quell all this protest or at least you know make it more peaceful. Portland was such a beautiful city and I got to see some of that. We had a couple sunshiny days, little bit of rain, of course, but you know I have some wonderful memories of the way the city used to be. It was a nice place to grow up."

That stopped Kate's excitement. She didn't like the fact that Tyler was feeling an attachment to his old hometown. Of course she had an attachment to Sonoma County where she was raised, but it put her on red alert and perhaps he wasn't telling her exactly what he was thinking, but it did open the possibility that he was considering joining the group at Bone Frog, like Gretchen had mentioned.

"Gretchen says that Trace is seriously considering the job offer he'd received. I know we talked about you interviewing with him, but honestly with all this going on with your parents I kind of thought that went out the window. Does this mean you changed your idea a bit?" she asked.

"Well, like I said on the phone, we do need to sit and talk, Kate. I want to make sure that I do the right thing. I'm not going to do anything that you're going to have a problem with. And I'm assuming you'll be the same way, right?"

"Of course, I think we can both figure out what's the right path for us. But I want to put a pitch in for us working together on something."

"I'm open to anything, as long as we thoroughly explore what those things are. But no worries." He smiled and leaned over to her, putting his right hand on her shoulder, pulling her toward him so he could give her a kiss. He quickly refocused on his driving as they swerved slightly, generating some neighborly honks from passing drivers.

After they pulled up to the school, Kate got out to go pick up Oliver. Grady would be returning home with one of his friends as part of the carpool. Oliver was burdened with several paintings, and a note that was safety-pinned to the front of his shirt. He looked funny trying to juggle all his things, all his prizes he wanted to show his mom and dad.

"Hey there bud. I missed you," said Tyler to his son.

"I made all these paintings for you, Dad." He shoved the crinkled paper in Tyler's chest, releasing them at the last minute. Kate watched as they fell to the ground and started floating all over the yard.

"Whoa there! Hey buddy, we got to pick these up before they get wet. Come on, help me," Tyler said to him.

Kate watched the two of them run around picking up the papers, as well as the brown paper bag that had some of his craft items in it and some paperwork from the school district. All of that was brought inside the

Suburban, Oliver was strapped in next to Kendall, and Tyler resumed the drive home.

She smiled as she looked at the face of her husband. How lucky she was. How lucky they all were. She hoped that it always remained this way.

CHAPTER 11

ALL OF TYLER'S concerns about Kate, about their future, melted away in their long and patient lovemaking that evening. The one thing that he appreciated about Kate more than anyone else he'd ever cared about, was that she was not afraid to show him how she felt. It had been a leap of faith for her to fall in love with him in the first place, being engaged to someone else when they met on the plane that fateful afternoon. He knew something about her was what he'd been looking for his whole life. And although they'd had their differences over the years, the last ten years since being married and the birth of their three children, had only deepened his desire and respect for her.

Now it was all about making sure neither one of them caved in or settled for second, since they both were in effect racehorses. Neither one of them were plodders. Neither one of them wanted a life that was just ordinary. Tyler had always been someone with stars in his eyes and a tremendous amount of drive in his soul to protect the whole fucking world. He laughed to himself as he kissed her smooth skin and luxuriated in the smell of this divine woman, he was lucky to have love him. He never forgot that and never stopped being grateful for it.

But Kate on her own, also was a racehorse. She wanted things in her life to be perfect. She wanted to be a great mother, she wanted to be a strong partner for him, always supporting him. And even though sometimes they'd get tired, or the stress of life, or him being gone for long periods of time, especially when the kids got sick or there was a money issue, all these stressors would wear her down when he wasn't home sometimes. Or sometimes when he was home and he was spending more time with the team than he was spending with her or the kids. There were always things coming up that wore on them, both of them.

But it was always their love that took front and center stage. It was like when they met each other they found someone else that could do great things with their life, but not forget their commitment and the power of the love they shared between them as primary. In fact, all of his strength now came from that love. He would be devastated without her.

As he explored and worked on all the little things

he knew she loved as they made love, the way she liked to take it slow and have her orgasm build, build until she had no control, because for Kate, losing control in this positive way, was refreshing and needed. It wasn't the frantic kind of losing control when your whole world is exploding. He wanted her to let go, to shatter beneath him, to give him back what she felt and all the intensity of the love she felt for him. She was always willing to give her very best all the time.

He chastised himself a little bit, maybe just began worrying about it, as he was making love to her how could he be thinking about all these other things? And he decided that it was part of who they were as a couple. They were entangled just as they'd been entangled in bed, couldn't help themselves, jumped over boundaries that other people would never do, this was their life. And loving her body, loving her soul, loving the way she loved him back, that was what he wanted and that's what she wanted too. So he felt for her, felt the love and the desire physically with his body, but he also understood that love. It wasn't just sex, it wasn't just passion, it was how she loved him back, how he loved her.

"I wish I didn't ever have to leave your side, Kate. And that's probably pure folly. I want you to know that I miss you, I even miss you when I leave to go to team meetings. I miss you when I take the kids to school. I can't wait to see you every time I come home," he said to her.

Her face was still sweaty from her fitful orgasm, her breathing still ragged, deep, her eyes nearly delirious. He loved seeing in her eyes how his words affected her all the way to her core. He traced her lips with his finger, kissed her again whispered in her ear, "I love you so much, Kate."

"I am the lucky one, Tyler," she whispered back. "I think about it every day, what would've happened if I hadn't trusted myself enough to know the difference between where I was headed and what significance meeting you on the plane caused for me. You made my life a miracle. It was fate all the way from start to finish. And we're not done yet." She said and smiled.

"It's an adventure right? That's what they say about love, it's the best suspense out there. It's a mystery, just like any good mystery story. The love is the mystery, how it unfolds. And for me, I know it grows stronger every year we're together. And now I see the kids growing, some of you and some of me, the blending of our personalities, and the way they honor us as our children, because their hearts are pure, I can't tell you what joy it brings me. And I know it's a lot of work on you when I'm gone, but I want you to know I appreciate it so much. I look into the eyes of our three, and I see your magic in their eyes too, Kate."

Of course, her eyes teared up, because Tyler's eyes were tearing up. He felt his tears stream over his cheeks and down onto his bare chest. God help him, he wanted this relationship to last forever. He wanted to live forever in her arms.

IN THE MORNING, Tyler was grateful she didn't force the serious discussions about their future on him last night. Now, having coffee in bed after another quickie encounter, her lying tangled in the sheets still naked, and the room still smelling of her and their lovemaking, he sat with the two mugs heavy in whipping cream, presented it to her, and decided to flay open his soul.

"I know what you did last night, Kate."

Kate looked puzzled as she sipped her first sip and then closed her eyes and licked her lips. "Mm, this is the best coffee you've ever made."

Tyler thought about that. "This is the best morning of my life. I am so lucky, Kate. Honest. But I still know what you did."

He tried to look serious, maybe even alarm her slightly but he had to break out in a chuckle as she began to worry.

"I'm not sure what you're saying, Tyler."

"I want you to know that I'm willing to have that discussion this morning about whether or not I'm going to leave the Teams. I know you've worried about it. So can we do that? And Honey if you don't want to, I'm fine with that. But I feel like I promised, and I put you off on that phone call which I really am sorry for, and now I need to keep my promise. So here I am, let me have it."

She looked at him over the rim of the coffee mug. "Be careful what you wish for Mr. Gray."

"Are you going to do a 50 Shades on me then?" he said.

"Let me put it to you this way." She adjusted herself, coming up to sit, her knees and legs wrapped around her torso, the sheet pulled up to cover her breasts, but her lovely arms and fingers that held the coffee cup could have just as well been holding Tyler's heart the way he felt for her. He was addicted to her inside, outside, in the air, everything that she touched or breathed he loved. There would never be a time that he wasn't devoted to her.

"Yes? I'm waiting," he said.

"I first want you to know that I am worried about you taking your next step, because I know you get so much satisfaction out of what you do, even with all the dangers, because that's just the way you were made. It's the way you do everything, you do it full tilt, all out, no reservations. And while neither one of us are perfect, you have so much discipline and training, it comes natural to you."

"Well, I think you're the same way, Kate."

"No, not exactly the same way. I try to figure things out too, but I am driven more by inspiration. I like to do things that make me feel good. Like this catering business, like raising the children, like gardening. Like making the house a beautiful place, those are things that bring me joy, they bring me energy pennies."

"Energy pennies not energy silver dollars?" He asked, playing with her.

"No, I got that from someone I've heard speak about it, and it's energy pennies, doing things that put something back into your vessel." She said this while tapping at her chest. "Inspiration is my motivation, to create beauty and health in abundance. I'm not sure it's inspiration for you, but you are driven to protect and to keep safe and to cherish. It's a different thing."

"And is there something wrong with that difference between us?" He wondered.

"No, not at all. But I have to understand your motivation just like you have to understand mine. And if we are going to do something together it has to include both of those things for us to work together as a team. We do that in raising our family now, Tyler. You protect and provide for us, I watch over the kids and keep them safe and make the house a home and keep the home fires burning so when you come back you don't have to be handling projects or problems that I haven't taken care of. That's the beauty of how we work together in raising this family, in having this partnership. Because a marriage really is a partnership isn't it?"

"Yes it is. I never thought about this the way you are. So what you're saying is my need to protect and defend is part of what I should be doing if I'm no longer on the Teams, is that what you're saying?"

"I think yes, and that can take many forms. If we do something together, you have to be able to live in that world and love it, while I'm living in my world and loving it. And that's what we both bring to the partnership outside of the family and the marriage. And if it's done right, it can be a great enhancement. I don't want to take you away from your brothers, and I see things and I hear things and I've heard wives that do nothing but complain about you guys. I understand what they're saying, and I probably think some of it's justified. But I can tell whether they are of one team, when some of these conversations come up and it turns into like a bitch session. Not all the wives do that and I've, for instance, never heard Christy do that. I don't know if the guys do, but I can tell which relationships are really working and which ones aren't. I would like to have the kind of relationship that works and I think we do have that, Tyler."

He was incredibly proud of her. The delivery was flawless. He wished he'd had a recording of what she said so he could just play it over again and again and again, especially if he was out in some distant area in the shivering cold or worrying about getting shot somewhere. He would love to be able to hear her voice like this, affirming the best parts of him and noticing the best parts of her.

"You're incredible Kate. How did I get so lucky?"

"You sat next to me, and you looked at me with those blue eyes, and you reached right in and grabbed my heart. You didn't even hesitate. And you didn't even act like you knew that's what you were doing. I didn't know what was going on. But something triggered in me and I knew from that day forward if I didn't follow you or follow my instinct to be with you, my life would never be the same. We were both lucky, Tyler."

"Okay so this is all good and nice, but how do we make that decision whether or not I stay on the Teams are not?"

"Well, that is your world, and that is a decision you are going to have to make. Let me remind you about a few things. You've lost teammates, you've had teammates come back disabled, missing an arm or a couple of legs, blinded, severe cases of PTSD, some of them addicted to opioids and other drugs, coming back and making messes of their lives, getting divorced and financially in ruins. You've had all kinds of things in your Team and other Teams that you've seen. Accidents during training, being told by the Navy that you're no longer qualified. All these things can and do happen every day of every year. So we know that the longer you stay, the more chance this could happen. That doesn't mean you don't do it anymore, it just means that now you're 37 years old, you're not 27 years old and things happen to a 37-year-old body that perhaps don't happen as easily with a 27-year-old body. And now you have three little ones who you love dearly, that look up to you, and they'd survive, but they'd be devastated if you were harmed, or if you didn't come back. And I know you've seen those kids at SEAL funerals, you've seen the wives and the parents, you've seen the impact of all of that on the community. It's a question that only you can answer. I can't do that for you. I think you need to look at that first. I think that's where it has to start. And while you're doing that, I need to be thinking about what kind of an operation I could do perhaps on a limited basis until you are done with your commitment here, and whether or not I like it enough to even do it by myself if you decide you don't want to join me. The long and the short of it is, Tyler, I don't want to have you leave the Teams and then find out later that you gave up your whole life. I want you to be with me the best version of yourself that you possibly could be. I don't want you to hold back. I want you to take risks, but I want you to take calculated risks. I want you to love what you're doing, no matter what it is."

If he could bottle up her energy, her confidence, the love she held for him sitting sipping her coffee tangled in their bedsheets, stark naked, beautiful, lips that could sink a battleship, words that made his heart flutter, if he could just bottle it up and take a shower in it every single fucking day, he'd be a much better person.

Why did he worry so much about what she wanted or whether or not the changes were going to be good for them? If they just paid attention and moved from the point of what they loved doing, there wasn't anything in the world that could stop them.

CHAPTER 12

KATE AND TYLER decided that Kate should run up and spend a couple of days with Devon and Nick at the Winery and Lavender Farm in Sonoma County. That way, she could have some of her questions answered, and they could have another discussion about some of Kate's ideas before Tyler left for his deployment. Nick and Devon's kids were at camp, since it was spring break for them. Her kids were involved in several sporting events, and Tyler was prepared to handle all three of them. Although Oliver and Grady were in school, Kendall started a new preschool, which took three-year-olds, but with certain exceptions, would accept somebody younger if they were fully potty-trained. Tyler wound up enrolling her in the preschool that Kyle and Christy's kids went to, having remembered some of the programs that school provided that he liked. That also gave him more leeway in the workups and meetings that they had, freeing him up a little bit.

Kate flew up on a Wednesday, planning to return on Saturday. They were still waiting for further information from the adjuster and the insurance company, so it was a small break in the all-consuming disaster and resolution project that had been Portland. They both decided not to overly pepper Larry and Deidre, Tyler's parents, about moving. They were experiencing some resistance there.

Devon picked Kate up at the Sonoma County Airport, named after the famous artist, Charles Schulz.

"I forgot how beautiful it is up here, Devon. I mean, we fly in and it's green and with the beautiful vineyards dotting the landscape everywhere. I love it in San Diego, of course, but it's just so lush and gorgeous up here. I'm really excited."

"Well, I am delighted that you even want to come and talk to us about what you want to do. Of course, there's a part of me that hopes that you decide you can't do it on your own, and you agree to come here and stay and help us. You know that option's still out there for you." Devon said.

They drove down the freeway until a turnoff to Bennett Valley Road and the winery site.

"I think one of the biggest decisions we have to make is what's best for the kids too, Devon. They are pretty connected down there, and I don't know if I have the heart to dislodge them. But you know, they'll be out of the house in another 10 years and we'll probably be in a different situation."

"But what are you going to do in the meantime? Has he made a decision?"

"I'm leaving it up to him. But the answer is no, not yet."

"Well, the event center is, as you know, our biggest source of income. The winery is great and with the additional acreage we were able to get from our neighbor, we've got it planted, because all of his vines had to be removed, they were diseased and half of them were dead anyway from his lack of water. But we've put in some good varietals as well as a good healthy dose of Merlot, which we're known for here, and it's going to be six, seven years before we're going to see anything for it. So it's good that you're coming now, you can see what it's like at the beginning, if you decide you want to do a winery down there. I know the weather will allow it, but you're going to have to grow different things. And as far as setting up a center, well, I will show you everything we do, and I'll tell you about some of the things I'd like to do if we had unlimited resources."

"That's good. I want to see what you would do if you had unlimited resources. I'm sure it would be pretty fantastic." Kate said.

They both laughed.

"But you know reality is reality. Gravity is gravity. What goes up does come down, and if you make mistakes, you pay for it. That said, I wouldn't have it any other way. But the climate here as far as what you can do with your land is perhaps a little bit restrictive and becoming more restrictive every day."

"What do you mean, Devon?"

"We have rules placed on us now as far as the event center and having tastings and parties that weren't in place when we first started. In fact, I don't think we would've been allowed to have a winery here, on the edge of town, encroaching on housing. And of course the big buzzword here is low-cost housing or low-income housing. I mean, a lot of our political leaders would like us to just rip out everything and put in apartments. And you and I both know what that would look like."

"I see what you mean. So you're saying nothing stays the same. It's always changing." Kate answered.

"You got it. That's lesson number one. And you got it Kate."

They drove down Bennett Valley Road until they got to Sophie's Choice, the Lavender Farm and Winery. Driving down the gravel road, lined in yellow roses, the vines leafing out and beginning to spread, the floor of the vineyards well tilled, the rich dark brown soil warmed by the afternoon sun, she imagined that a couple of centuries ago when the first settlers came out from wine-producing regions in France and Germany, they saw this as a true paradise.

It was a spiritual experience for Kate. She had enjoyed working at Heller Winery prior to moving to San Diego, but had never really been involved in the day-to-day operations. She was just part of the management team that ran the event center. They were strictly a winery, not an eco-tourist place, and not a wedding center. Although they did occasionally have weddings there. Most of her experiences were selling club memberships and catering to tourists who had no clue about what they were tasting. Her goal was trying to convert a few of them to being long-term buyers of the wine.

What Devon and Nick were doing was something entirely different. She wondered, if she had married Randy and involved in the winery, would she have taken them to a different place? She decided to pose the question to Devon.

"Do you ever wonder why somebody like Randy's parents didn't create something like this with their winery? They certainly have the room, they have the name, you would think they would try to do something like this and expand into more of the experience. That and the fact they're in Dry Creek Valley for starters. It's world famous."

"I'm not sure about them. You heard the news, didn't you?"

"No, what?"

"Well, as you know, their former employee left with hundreds of thousands of dollars. They found even more things after she was captured, and then just three weeks ago she was released, all charges dropped. None of us can figure out why. Mrs. Heller has had a recurrence of her breast cancer, and she's bedridden. Mr. Heller, I think, has taken his eye off the ball a bit, because the vineyard is in terrible shape. Randy's trying to do what he can, but he is such a mess. He's been married and divorced twice now, and I just don't think he's a very good business person. Everybody's talking about the fact that the vineyard's going to be for sale. I'm sure it's going to be many, many millions of dollars, and Nick and I wouldn't have anywhere close to the resources, nor would we really want to take it over. But people are starting to show up, and the wolves are coming out."

"That's a shame. That wine was just fantastic. I mean, they won so many medals."

"Well, their old reputation isn't helping now, because I guess they've lost several winemakers over the years. I think they are running short of funds. They were concerned about losing the business altogether from what I understand, but they were able to get some investors in and it just didn't get managed properly. I don't know why they lost interest, but there's something about this investor pull that has kind of taken the fire out of the bellies of the Hellers. I think they're not long for this area. I expect that they'll be moving somewhere else and selling."

"That's amazing. So why did they let Sheila go? I mean, why did they release Sheila?

"You mean Joan? That's her real name, you know. Joan?"

"Yes, she tried to kill me. The trial was over, she was serving time, I thought everything was settled. Why would they turn her loose?"

"Well, somebody has messed up what's going on and apparently some people who were witnesses or had testified against her are now changing their story. She's apparently claimed that someone else put her up to it, I don't know. But they let her go. And nobody's seen her, so she's not around the winery at all, not around Randy I mean, that lasted like a hot minute."

"Oh I knew that. That happened before she was convicted," said Kate.

"Well, she's onto other things. The $400,000 or whatever it was, plus the new stuff they found, was never seized. She was never required to turn it back or didn't have it. It's hard to get the straight story from the news media, but it's just a big puzzle. She's gone. She's gone with the money, the Hellers are failing, and everything about their life has just gone to pot."

"That's too bad. No, I didn't know anything about it. Do you think my folks know? They never said anything to me. And we've been up here visiting."

"This industry of ours is a very close and incestuous type of group, gossip and insider information is just all over the place. Some of it's accurate, most of it is not, so I don't really know that I've got the straight story either, but they try to keep it all within this group and if it wasn't for the fact that we attend some of the same meetings and some of us have used the same accountants and attorneys and salespeople, services, word gets out. And we've also interviewed a few of their employees for work at our place. I'm telling you, Kate, it's a hellhole. And I don't even know how much control the Hellers have. Because they completely rebuilt that place and it looks like a great big warehouse. It lost all the charm after the fire. It's just a metal building with a tasting room. I mean, who would want to have a wedding there?"

"I suppose there's some kind of a business model for somebody who's the investor but I agree with you, nothing I'd want to be involved in."

Kate didn't want to say it but she thanked her lucky stars she never did.

AFTER KATE AND Devon arrived, she was shown to her bedroom, and Nick appeared at the doorway, greeting her. She was unpacking and pulling out a couple of trays she had brought from San Diego as a gift.

"Hey there Kate, now I'm asking myself why the heck didn't you just bring the whole family? I mean, we could put them to work."

Kate ran over to him and gave him a deep hug. "Great to see you, Nick. I understand things are going very well for you guys. And I'm so happy."

"Well, the kids are going to be excited to see you and I'm busy that's true, but gosh that guy Tyler, he slips through town and he doesn't stop and come in and see me, I'm going to get after that guy. And I understand he's considering leaving the teams, which I can wholeheartedly accept, so when's the date?"

Kate knew she had to straighten this out. "Actually, Nick, he hasn't made that decision yet. We want to make sure it's the right decision before we do it."

"Well, maybe you ought to just make it easy and come up here and help us. You know, join in with us. We'd love to have you guys."

"As you've told us many, many times, Nick. But I'm afraid even I can't make that decision for him. It's something he must do on his own. And if he doesn't make up his mind for another month or two, even if he comes back and hasn't resigned, I'm just not going to push him. I think we've come to a really great understanding, and it's more important that it's the right decision and something that we don't rush into."

"Sounds good to me."

"I was really surprised to hear about the Hellers. Do you know anything different about the situation, and the release of Sheila, or Joan, her real name?"

"No, it is kind of a mystery. I'm sure eventually we will. It just happened, you know just what, two, three weeks ago? I know they're still looking for her and unless they bring additional charges, she was released on time served. Apparently there were defects in the charging that made it so that she has in fact served the minimum amount of time and was able to be released. I don't know how they make these determinations. I'm glad I'm not the person in charge, but that's the way it wound up being. And thank God, they say she's left our area. Let her go prey on somebody else."

"That's just amazing. I can't believe it. Well, that doesn't really affect us. I'm just here to soak up what you know, take it back to San Diego and present the facts, make my case with my husband, and hopefully we can come to some kind of a conclusion and a compromise that'll work for both of us. And of course you heard about his parents, right?"

"Oh yeah, he called me about that. What a shame. I am so sorry for his mother especially. Her life's work up in smoke. I mean, I lived through the fire here at the winery. I don't ever want to do that again. I mean, if it happened to us again, I'd be done. I can't do it again."

"I think you'd find a way. After all, you have a piece of paradise here, don't you?"

Nick stood in the doorway with his arms crossed, scratching his chin with his fingers, a little sparkle to his eye.

"Yeah, it is paradise. And you're right, I would never let it slip away."

CHAPTER 13

GRADY HAD A baseball game after school, so Tyler took Oliver and Kendall, sat in the bleachers and cheered him on. He got three solid hits and played third base without an error. The team won by one of the runs that Grady hit into home.

The team afterwards were cheering and jumping for joy, as they so far had been undefeated. Plus, Grady's team was on average four to five inches per player shorter. The others weren't older, or at least they said they weren't, but Tyler suspected there was some funny business going on and some birthdates were altered.

The coach for their Giant's team came up to Tyler afterward, shaking his hand. "We would sure be obliged if you would help us out with the training next year. I mean we're looking through the season and figuring we're going to place pretty high, so there'll be a lot of kids wanting to get on the team. I just would love to have an additional coach, and with your athletic experience and you being a hero, we just thought it would be wonderful if you could help out. And we understand you have to be gone for long periods of time."

"Well, that's an honor, sir. I'll see what I can do. I always make it a habit not to promise anything until I check with my better half, though. She may have other plans for me."

The coach chuckled. "I'm sure she does!"

The kids wanted to go for ice cream, and although they hadn't eaten first, Tyler relented. He took them to their favorite custard shop, and all of them, including Kendall, got a single scoop with sprinkles on top. It had been quite a process to get Kendall to agree to something, she wanted to have them all, but at the end, she elected for the same combination that her two older brothers did.

They came home for dinner, Tyler having put together some of the things that Kate had set aside and frozen in advance, a nice macaroni and cheese mixture with bacon, which was one of their favorites. He sat down with them and had a salad himself, and a small piece of steak from the night before. He made sure afterwards that they got cleaned up, that they changed into their pajamas and did homework for Grady, Oliver and Kendall were given books to read. No TV.

That was a sore subject but they agreed in the end.

It had been a good day, Tyler had made several phone calls, he'd been able to have a workout down at the Team room, Kendall was enjoying her preschool, although it was only two and a half hours long, but she loved the other kids and the teachers. That was making him happy that she had something other than just being home alone with him to occupy her day. He felt it was good for her.

He updated Kyle on what he knew, called his parents and didn't get an answer. Then he called the insurance adjuster.

"I'm sorry I don't have numbers for you yet. The insurance company's kind of dragging their feet though. Not like them. I'll try to get something for you and give you a call by the end of the day."

Well, since that didn't happen, and as life seemed to click away, the minutes and hours of the day were gone, and Tyler knew he'd have to call them tomorrow.

He dialed Kate to check in on how she was doing.

"Oh Tyler it's so beautiful up here. I'd forgotten how pretty it was. I've gotten a lot of information just from talking to Devon and Nick this evening and I got a good tour of the facilities. Tomorrow we're going to go over all the books and how they handle the bookings, how they do their ordering and hiring. It's really a work of love for them, and I didn't realize that they actually make more money on the event center than they do the winery."

"That makes perfect sense. I know they always say if you want to make a small fortune in wineries start with a big fortune. But I know it takes a while to get going. They've been around over 10 years now though, it should be starting to take hold."

"Well, remember they bought the new property last year and it does take six, seven, maybe eight years to have a full harvest out of new vines. And they've gambled on the varieties. There's a lot to wine making that I never realized. Oh, and the Hellers have just more or less imploded on themselves. They're in horrible shape I guess."

"Really? How so?"

"They took on partners to try to stay afloat after the theft of all that money, and I guess missus is sick again with her cancer. Randy's been trying to run the winery but he's proving to be a very incompetent manager, which I could have told them."

"No kidding. I wouldn't put him in charge of anything. Not even the wait staff or the trimming crew."

"Well, here's the other thing, they've released Sheila from prison. Apparently, she was sent up north to some super-max prison? But something was discovered with her case, and she was released. They said she'd already served her time. I think she only served seven years."

"All that money and she only served seven years?"

"It was some kind of an error with the judge's charging orders, a technicality, and she got a good attorney, and that's what happened. She's off. She's free."

Tyler heard the little bells and whistles going off in the back of his head. "So where is she?"

"Nobody's seen her. Nobody knows. She doesn't have any probationary period, so she doesn't have to check in with anyone. Except for the fact there's still an ongoing investigation as to where the funds are, which she claims she doesn't have and always claimed somebody else had put her up to it, there isn't anything they can hold her on until they have proof. And that's the problem."

"Wow. That's one dangerous person out there. She's a really good con artist. One of the best I've met. I wonder what the hell she's up to."

"Well, apparently, she's made some friends, because her connections helped her get that high-priced attorney and get her off the hook, and she's not doing anything as far as anyone knows. But as long as she stays out of everybody's way, hopefully the Hellers will win out the suit on the insurance claim, which is still ongoing. Devon told me there was some talk about Sheila claiming that money because of her wrongful prosecution, although that hasn't been ruled. She's just been released for lack of evidence. So she's sticking with it all until the Hellers are driven into the ground."

"She's diabolical. They weren't saints, but they didn't deserve that. What a vampire."

"I could see how Mr. Heller would be despondent. Not helping Mrs. Heller with her cancer either. All this has just killed the two of them. So unfair."

"And yet, they caused some of this themselves," Tyler said.

"It's true. Came out of pure hubris. Remember when they thought they could order everyone around?"

"There's a saying about that."

"Been a problem for them financially. But maybe eventually they'll get paid off. In the meantime, they have partners that have rebuilt the place and it looks terrible—at least that's according to Devon. I'm not going to set foot on that property ever again."

"That's my girl. You stay as far away from Randy Heller and his family or anyone associated with that winery. And Kate, if you see Sheila, you stay away from her too. Now that she's out and about, that kind of gives me a whole new perspective on my parents' fire. Do you suppose she would stoop to something like that? I mean you were friends with her for several years."

"Tyler, I don't even know if I ever really knew her.

She's an odd duck, and has just strange reactions to things. I mean look at how she went off on me to try to get to you. She's just odd and damaged somehow. And blames everybody else I guess. Now going after the Hellers when she was the one who caused their demise in the first place. Give that woman some money, and you're right, she's almost evil. Dangerous is too mild a word."

"Like I said, stay clear away. If you see her, let me know right away."

"I've washed that whole scenario of what we went through 10 years ago, I've washed that out of my system. I don't spend any time thinking about it."

"Well, that's probably good. But keep a lookout for any little sign that doesn't make sense. You may be done with her. Maybe she won't be done with you, and she knows a lot about you, Kate. Look at what she tried to do with me?

"You're right. I promise."

"I need to check with the investigators then and maybe give them a heads-up. Thanks for that, and just remember, I can't wait till you come home on Saturday."

"Me too."

"Oh I almost forgot. Grady's team won tonight. They're so excited, that makes them undefeated. And this was the best team in their league so they have high hopes for taking the championship. The coach has asked me to help with the coaching next year. I told them I would have to check with my business manager, you."

"Thanks, Sweetheart. Say, I've got to run, but I'll check in with you before I come home. In the meantime I'm safe, I'm having a great time, I just love your friends Devon and Nick. They've treated me like a queen. Nick even asked why I didn't bring the whole family. I think the next time I'd like to do that if you're up for it."

"We'll get our calendars cleared out so we can do that. Maybe after I get back from deployment. We need to have a nice long trip to wine country. I know you'd enjoy it, it'd be great to see your parents, and there's lots of fun stuff to do. But you take care and stay safe, and don't go streaking off doing anything on your own okay?"

"Yes sir. Roger that!"

Tyler placed a call to the investigator he had spoken to at the site, and had several follow-up calls with.

"I just wanted to let you know that someone from our past, a woman who professionally embezzled I think over a half a million dollars from this winery in Santa Rosa, has been released unexpectedly and was in one of your prisons in the north, my wife said it was a maximum-security prison, and I am just calling to let you know that she's been released about three weeks ago and kind of has an ax to grind against our family, but mostly me. However, she did exhibit some rather dangerous behavior against my wife, and I don't know if this would have anything to do with the arson, but I sure would like it if you would add that to your list of things to check out."

"What's her name?"

Tyler gave him her name, as well as the name she went by, and explained the two. "She's apparently made friends with certain people in prison, she never returned any of the money or they couldn't find it, as she claimed it was somebody else who was behind her thefts, but apparently she bought herself a high-powered attorney, which tells me she might still have access to the funds. And the fact that she's only served seven years out of a 15-year sentence, not because of good behavior but because of some kind of an error, that just smacks as something wrong. My wife just mentioned it to me or I would've told you earlier. We thought she was safely tucked away and wouldn't be a problem for years. I doubt though that the time in prison has made her any less ardent about coming after us. But maybe I'm just being paranoid."

"I remember that case, and I remember hearing that she'd been released too. But my understanding is she's sort of disappeared into the woodwork."

"That's what my wife understands as well. There was some talk when she was behind bars that she would go after the owners' insurance claim, if you can believe such a thing. Just when I thought I'd heard it all, something like this happens, and makes me wonder."

"Yeah, try being in my line of work. You see much more than you ever wanted to."

"Please, just put your feelers out to check it and see what you come up with. I know you can't divulge everything, but let me know if there's anything else I can shed light or background on, and I just would be curious if you have any sightings or anyone has had any communication with her or her attorney."

"Who's her attorney?"

"I have no idea. I'm sure you could find it in the record, but nobody informed us, reached out to us, and I don't even think Mom and Dad know. I'm going to call them so they know that Sheila's been released, just in case they see her. It would surprise my mother especially if she was on the street. And I don't think she'd stay anywhere close to where the prison is so she's probably long gone. But I just want you to know."

"Thanks Tyler. I'll put the word out. You take care then."

CHAPTER 14

K ATE AND DEVON poured over the websites Devon used to advertise the wedding center, also showed her a list of vendors that she had cultivated over the years running the place.

"You want to have a newsletter sent out to all your former attendees. When they do make reservations online, we get their email addresses and ask their permission to be placed on the list. We also give referrals to people who refer others to our center, and that has really generated a lot of business, because families of families who have attended here love it and then want to use it for their wedding sometimes years later."

"Got it," Kate said. "Makes total sense."

"The winery is a different story altogether and it's not as fan-based run as the wedding center. So in that event we have our winemaker help us to enter into contests and things so we can get recognition and notoriety. We do every celebrity chef-type activity in Sonoma County we can, any wine tasting that we can be invited to, we do. I think it's very important that we both are the front and center spokesman for the winery, the lavender farm, and for the events center. And one kind of cross pollinates the other."

"What do you mean by that?" asked Kate.

"Well, when we're at a tasting event, we're also advertising the wedding center. When we're doing the wedding and taking reservations for that we make them an offer to use our wines at a discount, so that it's in essence a wine tasting for a captive audience while they're at the event. And one does compliment the other. The lavender farm we have contracted with a group of women who have a nonprofit setting up homes for battered women or women with children or women with young babies, and I've allowed the proceeds from that, and they're not tremendous, but it's something, we've allowed the proceeds to be a write off for us and allowed the ladies to use our lavender to make their oils and creams and sprays. It really does my heart good to do that for somebody, and it also is good for business. So it shows that we're trying to do good things for the county, for the area, and for these women in particular."

"I knew about the lavender farm, but I didn't realize you did that," said Kate. "I'm amazed at all of this,

Devon."

"Well, it's taken a while to build and to develop, and for a number of years you know we were wrapped up in this lawsuit with our neighbor. That kind of took us off track for a few years, but it's now solidified to the point that we are able to do solid growth every year, and barring any unusual event that would say wipe out our grapes or, you know, some weather event that would be difficult to absorb, the center still goes on. As you can see from my reservation list we're now booking things two years out. And those places have to pay in full at least 12 months in advance."

"So what happens if they decide not to get married, or they cancel for some reason?"

"That happens, and it's a case-by-case basis. If it's a hardship where one of the parties is ill or has passed away and that's happened to us unfortunately, or perhaps the parents have fallen on hard times and the money is not there to complete what they had promised their son or daughter, those are hardships that are tough. Now if it's a case of the couple behaving badly and being children, or parents trying to book something to lock them into a wedding, and you know, we see that all the time, we really do, it's a different story."

"But you charge for it, right?"

"Yes, we always do charge a cancellation fee, but we don't ever keep all of their money. That's just not fair and it causes too much ill will. There are some places that do though, and some of the big hotel chains are not very good about releasing people from their obligations. But we try to work it on a case-by-case basis and give them terms or give them a discount so that they can still go forward and have the event but have it impact them less. You know, at the end of the day, we're all people in this together, and you won't get referrals if you treat people poorly."

"Okay so I see you've got these sites. These are pre-made websites that you can lock into?"

"Yes, there are a number of wedding shows, wedding programs, there are many places where you can advertise, I mean, we could spend a fortune on advertising and we do as much as we can, but we don't want to get overloaded. We attend all of these shows, we've tried to get a film crew here to do a destination wedding type of project, but so far that's still in the works and hasn't come to fruition. But you can see we've got like 15 or 20 places we can advertise online and just like Vrbo, they can click through and see the different places. Some of these sites are even international, so you're getting people from all over the world who want to come to Sonoma County and book a site. When we first started, this wasn't as extensive. But now, with the absolute birth of all these destination wedding venues, people are building hotels next to wineries and doing all kinds of things to really enhance the whole experience."

"You make it look easy. A hotel? Like Hotel Dunn?"

"That will never happen. While that's not something we want to do, this is a growth industry. And there's no stopping it. Some people spend obscene amounts of money for their weddings. A little less for anniversaries."

Kate and Devon went through the bookings, how the bookings were handled, she showed Kate her website, she told Kate they even had a full-time website manager and reservation manager who monitored the traffic and made it so that Devon and Nick were not stuck on the computer all day long.

"That's a very important hire, when you get to the point where you're just going crazy and you can't handle everything, you have to make that hire very strategically, has to be somebody who's well-organized, who knows how to check things and gets right back to people. We get bookings because we contact people right away. You'd be surprised how many people just never get back to their clients and then a week or two later they've found another site. So it's a very important position."

She showed Kate into another office area.

"You can see the gal over here," Devon pointed to a

cubicle encased in glass, where a young woman was sitting at a desk with two large screens side by side, a pair of headphones and microphone on her head.

"Molly is our go-to gal, and she also majored in computer science in college, so she was a great find, and she loves doing this job. In fact, she doesn't want to expand her operation at all, doesn't want to take on additional duties, and we'd probably give it to her if she wanted. But we're happy with her, we're not going to mess with success."

Kate wanted to visit her mother and she asked if Devon would like to come.

"I'm afraid I can't, I've got too much to do here. But you can borrow my car and go see her if you like. I'm just not going to be available, and I have to do some errands downtown."

"Why don't I agree to meet you somewhere, and we'll have lunch then?"

"Okay, I'll drive one of the company trucks then and I'll meet you."

They chose a small delicatessen downtown that had been one of Kate's favorites growing up.

After visiting her mother and father, Kate headed for the late luncheon with Devon. Walking up and down the downtown area of Santa Rosa, Kate was flooded with past memories of her childhood, her high school years, and her early years working for Heller

Winery. She remembered her first pair of tennies and colorful socks she bought from the eclectic gift center catering to teens. The used record store was gone, but in its place, was a nail bar and beauty salon. A couple of Shabby Chic designer stores sat side by side, as well as a bunch of new bistros, wine bars and children's clothing outlets.

She knew she wouldn't recognize anyone, and most of the stores were new to her. There were a few more boarded-up businesses than she had remembered, and a few more people hanging out in the park than she'd remembered. But all in all, it was nothing like the Portland scene. And she hoped it never would be.

Out on the patio of the deli, she got a table, had a light spritzer soda, and waited for Devon. About ten minutes later, she arrived.

"Wow what a morning. I just got back from the insurance company and it looks like we're going to be saving some money on our insurance because of our lack of claims. And that's such good news because it's a huge cost to us," said Devon. She sat and leaned into the table.

"I haven't ordered yet so choose whatever you like. It's on me."

"So how do you like downtown Santa Rosa? Does it bring back memories?"

"Oh of course it does. I am accustomed to San Diego now though, and it feels like home, mostly because the kids feel like it's their home. It took me a while though. This was a beautiful place to grow up. I don't regret living here at all."

"That's what I thought too. I mean we looked at other places and we thought, oh maybe we should go up north or maybe we should go south, maybe we should even consider going down there to San Diego, but with my business also real estate, which is now kind of phasing out—I've turned a lot of things over to another agent in the office—I work with some of my key clients on very large projects, but I wouldn't have that additional business. Now that the winery and center has taken off, I can give up some of that and it won't impact our future. It's kind of nice when you can transition from something you loved but had to do into something you love and love to do."

"That's what I'm looking for, Devon. And thanks for all this. It's been an eye-opener. I see how you do this, and I see what a difference it's made for you guys, and I'm just amazed at your operation. Nice thing is that you do most of it, don't you?"

"I wouldn't say that. Nick is in charge of all the work, the labor part of things. I just manage the publicity, the books, the office and the customer relations. In a way, it was something I was always good at before when I did real estate full time."

"I would not have known there was so much to do."

"You'll do it your way, Kate, if you do it. And you know, I have to say it, the opportunity is still there for you to come in and join us. Never feel like you have to be a stranger."

They started reviewing the menu when a shadow fell over Kate's end of the table. Looking up, she stared into the red rheumy eyes of her former fiancé, Randy Heller.

"Oh my gosh!" she said, startled. And then she realized she shouldn't have reacted so strongly, but the fear was real. She looked at Devon, who was puzzled and turned to see Randy, and quickly turned around and kept her back to him. Devon watched Kate carefully as if looking for a sign they should leave.

"Randy you scared me I'm so sorry. And I just didn't expect to see you."

It was obvious he was drunk, smelled of urine, his clothes were disheveled, his hair was uncombed and looked like it had been uncombed for several days. He frankly looked like someone who slept in a park all day long, wasn't the son of a prominent winery owner. His pants were too long for his frame as his frame had gotten skinnier, he smiled a weak smile and revealed yellow, crusty teeth, which absolutely turned Kate's stomach.

His appearance reminded her of someone who might be asking for money at the side of a roadway, a supermarket.

"To the woman who ruined my life."

Kate reacted to this with a combination of offense and fear. It was such a wrong characterization. She couldn't let the comment go unchallenged.

"I wasn't the one that ruined your life, Randy. That was Sheila. Sheila did that to you and your family."

"But if you hadn't decided to break off the engagement, I would've never gotten involved with her."

She stiffened further. "Also not true. As I recall it a little differently, Randy, you told me you'd been involved with her before. Sheila is the one who stole all your money, and made your life hell. All I did was decide not to marry you. And I'm sorry if you blame me, but that's unwarranted."

"If you can sleep with yourself at night, I guess everything's okay." His voice wafted out into the ether, fading. Then he redirected to her. "You know that Mom's sick, right?"

"I've been told. I've also been told your dad's not doing well."

"No, they're not doing well at all. I'm not doing well, either."

"I am truly sorry. Your parents were very nice to me always. And none of my decisions had anything to do with you. They had more to do with where I wanted my life to go. I just changed my mind about it. But I worry about you, Randy, and I want you to know I did care deeply about you."

"But you didn't love me."

The waiter made a point to step in and insert himself in the conversation, probably watching the communication and the expression of the customers standing nearby. "Excuse me, sir, I'd like to ask you not to bother the customers please."

Kate was glad he was a rather tall, muscular man, easily outmatching whatever strength Randy had left. Randy smirked, shrugged his shoulders, and held up his right hand, twinkling his fingers in a silent goodbye. He turned around and left, disappearing around the corner.

Devon reacted first. "Oh my God, I had no idea it was that bad, Kate. What a mess he is."

"I think he's gotten into something, probably some substance abuse of some kind, and he's not himself. I mean, that's not the Randy I used to be in love with. That's a shell of a person. And I feel sorry for him, and I guess I do feel a little bad."

"Oh, absolutely not, Kate. He put you through a wringer. And the parents, pushing their way around, I heard your mother talk to them several times, and I even talked to Gretchen about it too. They were not exactly nice to you like you say they were."

"It doesn't matter now. It's just how they were. I'm sure they never expected to fall on such hard times. That's what happens when you get involved with a con artist. The real culprit in all this is Sheila. She's the one that should have paid. Everything she touches rots. I don't understand people like that."

"Don't be naive, Kate, you have to be careful. With all this going on, you need to distance yourself from all of it. Yes we care about our fellow human beings, but we have to stay away. And I'm sorry, but they chose the path they took. They have to have a certain amount of responsibility for it. Maybe Mr. Heller is not only saddened by his wife's illness, but he's probably very saddened by what's happened to Randy. You know every parent wants to do the best for their kids, and look at where they are now. That is a very heavy burden, but don't blame yourself, Kate, please don't blame yourself. It's not healthy."

Devon leaned across the table and took Kate's hand.

"It's the drugs, Devon. The drugs destroy everything. Everything good about a person. It sucks people dry. So sad."

"People who go that path are dangerous, Kate. They can't help but use and blame others. They need treatment, not your pity."

"I never thought I would see this creep into my life, I never thought I would experience this firsthand. This is always something that happens to somebody else, not me."

"But Kate, you know, in our community, we have lots of happy couples that wind up in some kind of trouble, sometimes he doesn't come home, sometimes there's injuries and the happy ever after doesn't happen for them. I think what I'm saying is you want to be careful, but you also don't want to forget to be grateful. We have the best life possible, Kate. We're married to heroes, to men we can count on, to men who will protect us. And yes, not every man is a hero, not every wife is a supporting loving wife, a good mother. But we have the best of what there is and I will always respect the years that Nick spent on the Teams, but I am so grateful he is done with that. And thank God he loves what he does now."

It gave Kate a lot to think about. The appearance of Randy took her appetite away, but she picked at her food a bit, and then their conversation just stopped. Her heart was broken, not because of what had happened in her life, but what had happened in their life. She felt sorry for him even though she probably shouldn't. She still did. She wished there was something she could do, but she also realized, if she did it would be violating her agreement with Tyler. There was no way in the world she was going to do that.

CHAPTER 15

TYLER BEGAN TO be concerned when he still could not reach his parents. He wanted to let them know about the possibility that Sheila was out there. He wished that he was in Portland to check on them physically, so he called the fire inspector and asked if they could do a welfare check or send somebody from the police department to do a welfare check on them.

"They're older, not elderly, but they've been through a lot. I would just appreciate it if one of your guys could go up there and just make sure they're okay. God forbid something would happen and they had a fall or one of them had a stroke and the other one got injured trying to take care of them."

"Do you go days without talking to them?"

"Of course. But right now, we're in the middle of this investigation. It's very unlike them to not answer my calls. And they know there's lots of people involved in this whole affair, so they would be by the phone.

That's just who they are." Tyler said.

"Were they planning on going anywhere?"

"No. Absolutely not. Also out of character."

"Okay. I think you have a valid point there. I'll send one of the deputies over to do a welfare check then, and I'll call you back."

"Thank you so much. And is there anything further about your investigation?"

"Well, the only thing that we are a little bit stumped about is the fact that several of the cameras in the warehouse district, and there weren't a lot of them, were disabled. It looks like they were taken offline the day before, which begins to look like a planned event, right?"

"Of course it does. And what about the suspect or suspects?"

"Well, the main suspect who was seen during the painting during the demonstration, and we don't have a picture of the suspect at the warehouse, but the suspect that was at the downtown demonstration was very slight, and wore all black, including a black beanie and a black face covering. I would even offer to say that it was probably a teenager of some kind or young man. It's just odd that we have only one person doing that and everybody else running around setting fires to garbage cans, bashing in windows, and shouting and carrying signs. This particular person was definitely laying the groundwork for a lot of future damage. And the face recognition software doesn't work when they cover up their faces, and they frequently use umbrellas to cover their actions as well, so it's even hard to assess their body type. But I'm still of the theory that this isn't a huge, organized effort, and I still think it's the work of one individual."

"So, can I ask you about the release of Sheila, the lady that was involved in the fraud and embezzlement of the winery in Santa Rosa, the lady who accosted my wife? Do you think she might have had something to do with this or could that figure in the movie be a woman, not a man?"

"You gave me the heads-up, and we are still investigating those possibilities, but at this point I don't think so. It's just not something we see every day. I think it's just some kid who's disgruntled. And somehow got access to the materials. I wouldn't go that far as to say there's some kind of big conspiracy going on. You want to be careful about that Mr. Gray. And our resources are limited, getting smaller by the day, unfortunately."

"I understand. Well, please, after you do the check, have my mother call me, so I don't worry so much? Otherwise, I'm going to be flying up there and I'm going to be your worst enemy."

He chuckled. "Well, you'd have to join the line,

son. I appreciate your tenacity and I'd probably be the same way if it was my parents, but please don't interfere with what we're trying to do. We're trying to do the best job possible. And there's a lot of loose ends here and unfortunately some politics involved as well."

Twenty minutes later, Tyler got the call he'd been dreading. "I'm sorry to tell you this, Mr. Gray, but your parents aren't at home. Now there is a vehicle there at the house. It's a small Volkswagen Bug, but it doesn't look like it operates. Do they have another vehicle that they could be using?"

Tyler gripped the side of the chair in the living room. His kids were running around the backyard having a normal day, and Tyler was all of a sudden descending into the pits of hell with worry and concern over his parents. And it wasn't only just over his parents, if there was something happening with them, it was only going to be a matter of time before it engulfed all of them.

"They have a van, a Volkswagen van, a vintage one. And that's what they use, I just don't understand, did it look like the house had been lived in?"

"Well, here's the thing, their cell phones were in the kitchen on chargers. It appears they left without taking them. That's damned odd, don't you think? With an investigation going on, why would they not bring their phones with them?"

"And the house, was it damaged at all or tossed or was it, were there dirty dishes?"

"No, everything looked clean and neat, it looked like their bed hadn't been slept in or maybe they just make their bed early in the morning when they get up, I don't know. The neighbors say they haven't seen them since yesterday morning and they did leave briefly in the van, and then came back, and then somebody came back late last night but nobody saw any lights on in the house and the van's gone this morning. So I am going to put out a request for all units to be on the lookout for the van, and I have one other thing I want to tell you about."

Tyler braced for the worst.

"Okay."

"Remember when you told me yesterday about the attorney that handled the charge for Sheila?"

"Yes, I do."

"Well, I checked the court records, and they've used a gentleman by the name of Gregory Poplin, who's a big wig attorney out of a firm back east somewhere, but he specializes in helping protestors beat convictions for damage and loitering and all of that stuff. You're going to love this. His parents served time for blowing up a bank building years ago when he was a baby."

"Oh shit."

"No kidding. He's also a homeless advocate, and he's been quite vocal and nasty to our local police force. She used him, partially funded by their Rights and Justice League, it's a group that helps bail out trespassers and people who are doing protests for certain causes. And they have every right to protest, but this group was selected to help people in that situation, especially those charged with violent insurrection."

"Great." Tyler was getting sicker by the minute.

"This gentleman did handle her case and was able to get her released. Now, normally he would cost a fortune to handle something like this, but with the foundation, she probably got some help. I don't like that he's involved in this, I don't think he's involved in anything criminally, but he represents a lot of people who we think have been involved in criminal work. So, it's possible that if there's talk about going after insurance proceeds for this winery like you told me yesterday, it's possible he's behind it. And what that means is Sheila may be local now. It may be that we're looking for her as well as whomever else was involved in this protest. And I hate to tell you this, Tyler. Because it opens up a whole new avenue of issues, I'm afraid I'm going to have to leave it in the FBI's hands— let their good people work on it. This is going way beyond what I can do."

Tyler was shaking when he hung up the call.

Even though the inspector had apologized, still offered to help on a limited basis, he just felt like his swim buddy had turfed the class and quit. He didn't have any allies left, at least not at first.

And then he thought about the Bone Frog Protection Group and the words Bryce had told him when he called him a few days ago. He picked up the phone and dialed his number.

At first, a recording came on the line, and then Bryce picked up.

"How you doing Tyler? Are things getting resolved?"

"As a matter of fact, I'm calling you, because I think I'm going to need your services. You were nice enough to offer, but I'm going to just get right down to it Bryce. I think my parents have been kidnapped. I haven't talked to them since the day before yesterday, and I just had the police go over and do a welfare check on them and they are not home. And they've also left their cell phones in the kitchen charging. That's not like them. I have a really bad feeling about it. I am about ready to jump on a plane and get up there but I have the kids and I promised that I wouldn't get involved. I promised Kyle, I promised Kate, I just need some help."

"Okay, man, we've got your back. I'm going to have

to do a full incident report."

Bryce began grilling him on all the details of what Tyler knew, what he'd been told, and the timing of everything.

"Is there anything new in the investigation that I should know about?"

"They've brought in the Feds."

"That's a good thing, Tyler. They have resources the locals, even big city locals, don't have. Anything else?"

He also filled him in on the past confrontation with Sheila, the Hellers and the attack on Kate.

"She's a very sly, shady character. She embezzled money from the winery where Kate worked and has almost put that winery out of business. She was convicted of embezzlement and was due to spend fifteen years in prison, but she's been released now in seven, and she was befriended by some individuals while incarcerated, and put in touch with a high-powered attorney who got everything dismissed. It looks like and just feels like her hand at play here."

"Wow, you got a lot going on there, Tyler. How the hell did you think you could help your folks out with all this?"

"At the time, it wasn't with all this. It was just a fire. But things have been developing quickly and as I started to learn more details, I got more and more concerned. I'm smart. I know when it's more than I can take on."

"Yup. That's what a smart man does. We have sources you don't have, can sometimes find things others miss. It's why business is booming. If it comes to that, we do hostage rescue, and negotiation, too. You know that."

"Of course you do. Now Bryce, I don't want to be a crazy conspiracy theorist, and that's what the local police and fire chief thinks of this theory, but you and I know when we have a gut feeling, a hunch, we have to follow it up. So I'm looking to you to jump in and see what you could find out about this attorney, about this person, and see if she's left any tracks or if there's any evidence at the house that my parents live in that would indicate where they are?"

"I'm happy to do so, Tyler. You stay put though, you don't want to jeopardize your career by jumping into something you can't do. That's why we're here. And I will get the guys together and we'll put together something, do a little bit of legwork. You let me know the instant you get a whiff of something going on I don't know about, you hear?"

"Okay, thanks man. I love you brother."

"Right back at you, Tyler. Don't worry until you have something to worry about. We're going to do whatever we can and even a little bit more."

CHAPTER 16

KATE'S UNEXPECTED MEETING with Randy still bothered her, even after several hours. It was a face-to-face confrontation with pure evil. He was a stranger to her, a dangerous one, too. He had fallen so fast, so hard, so far to the bottom, that it scared her. It also scared her that his once powerful family, although extremely obnoxious during their heyday, had lost nearly everything now, including their own health, their own family unit. It was such a shame, and she was filled with grief and sadness.

Life can be a fickle lover sometimes, she said to herself. It was a phrase Tyler had used many times. It demonstrated how differently people reacted to negative things: some leaned in and made things work, or lessened the blow with their attitude, and others allow the situation to ruin them.

She'd also read in a self-help book, "Circumstances don't make a person, they reveal a person." And that was equally true. Some people reacted to small hiccups like it was the end of the world, while others could manage something huge and devastating, and learn from it, heal from it.

She knew which personality trait Tyler was. She hoped she was the same.

The fact that he blamed her for his troubles was a complete surprise. It showed Kate how devoid of reality he really was. She had done everything she could to let him down nicely, but in hindsight, she knew all along that being beside him, with that family, was going to be a mistake. She had no idea how right she'd been. And that also scared her.

One thing was for sure, the only thing she wanted to do now was to go home. She'd done the investigation, enjoyed spending time with Devon and Nick, and could see herself running her own business, like Devon did, and it excited her. Everything was on a positive lane until she saw Randy. Was he some sort of soul sucker who liked to put clouds in everyone's day? His refusal to see his own flaws and choices made it so no one else around him could survive either. He was in a downward spiral until he crashed and burned. There was nothing for him now.

But she'd gotten her answer for now. She could see the possibilities available to her, but only if it was the right time. And the answer very clearly was that this wasn't that time. And although she could have been disappointed, she chose to be strong, to face it head-on, "live for another day," another one of her favorite sayings. Now was the time to just stay together as a family unit, strengthen that unit, and not make any big changes.

What was most important was to help Larry and Deidre figure out what the rest of their lives were going to be first before she really started making any big plans for her family. No matter what happened, if they came to San Diego, if they rebuilt in another area, or even rebuilt at that location—even if they had lost it all and wouldn't be able to rebuild—discovering the way of that and the impact it would have on the whole family had to come first. They still had lots of time to plan. And although Tyler was open to the possibility of leaving the Teams, she wasn't sure now that she wanted to even ask him to do that.

When she turned into the gravel driveway, her phone rang, and it was Tyler. Her heart fluttered and instantly she was energized, filled with joy.

"Oh, Sweetheart, it's so good to hear your voice. I have had one hell of a day," she said to him.

"Well, that makes two of us, Kate."

He was direct and wasn't looking for chit-chat.

"Look, I'm going to ask you if it would be possible for you to come home. There are some things that have come up."

Kate noticed how cold his voice was, and that scared her.

"What's happened, Tyler?"

"We can't find Mom and Dad. And we are now shifting into the mode that something has happened to them. And I hesitate to ask you this, Sweetheart but I just have to. I know I said I wouldn't get involved, but I just cannot stay down here and wait for other people to do things that I could do. I want to go find them, I want to be part of that process. I just would not live with myself if I didn't."

"Well, of course. I would expect nothing less, Tyler."

He sighed and finally answered her. "You don't know how much that relieves me. You know, I took an oath to you when I said that I would not get involved and would let the authorities handle this, and I promised Kyle as well, but this is turning out to be a real mess. Much bigger than I thought it was. And I kind of feel like I'm in the center of it, like I'm the center of the wheel, not responsible for things, but somehow everything goes through me. Like someone is using everybody else around me to get to me. Does that make sense?"

"It does. But wouldn't it be safer if you just stayed in San Diego, stayed out of it, out of their way?"

"Let's look at that for a second, Kate. Me staying safe while my parents could be in peril? You think I could let that happen? You know I couldn't."

"I got it. That was me not thinking. Of course, you have to go, and of course, I will come home. I'll be home tomorrow. I'll get a flight somehow even if I have to go to LA and take a bus home." She hesitated and then added, "But are you going to be there?"

"Well, that's the thing, Kate. I want to get up there as soon as I can. So what I was thinking is I would drop the kids off at Gretchen's, and Gretchen and Angela could watch them until you could get home. I'm afraid I won't be here when you get home. But I'll check in with you. I've got a whole team of guys that said they'd help me here, and Bryce and his team are up there combing around looking for clues, so we'll see what goes on, and hopefully, we'll be able to find out what's happened and who's involved and get them brought to justice. I just don't know how long it's going to take. It bothers me I can't make promises."

"I understand, Tyler. I really do. We'll be good. And don't worry about me. My afternoon was quite an eye-opener. I'm not quite sure I want to be looking at making other choices right now."

"I'm in the same boat, Sweetheart. Let's just get to a level playing field first. And then when we can, we'll make those decisions, okay?"

"You got it. I love you so much, Tyler. Please be safe."

"Now that's a promise I'm going to keep."

She couldn't help but be disappointed, but at least she would see the kids. Then her logical side kicked in. "Where are you going to stay? Do you have some place safe?"

"I wish you had seen the Riley Estate, it's a fortress. Bryce and a whole bunch of his guys are there, old teammates of mine, some from other teams, some from other special ops groups, and then I'm going to bring three or four guys from here. We'll all be together, just like when we do an op overseas, which is how we figure stuff out. Not only will it be safe, the combined use of our brainpower is how this mystery is going to be solved."

"Okay, God speed. And please let me know when you get there."

That settled it for Kate, and she was not displeased she had to go home early. She might have even requested that anyway. She was done for now, considering all the possibilities that could be. She wasn't ready to give up the dream, but the timing sucked completely. And until Tyler's parents were helped and found and escorted to safety, there wasn't going to be any talk of running a new business, risking money, or risking more than she had to spend.

Once inside Nick and Devon's house, she sought them both out. "It looks like there's a problem with Tyler's parents. They've gone missing," she said.

"Oh no!" screamed Devon.

Nick was stoic in his answer. "That's not good."

"I'm going to try to get a standby flight out if I can tonight or tomorrow."

"So Tyler's going up there tonight?" Nick asked.

"Yes."

"And he's taking guys too, I'll bet."

"Yes, he said so."

"Where are the kids going to be?" asked Devon.

"They'll be at Gretchen's, until I get there. So I just need to find a flight, the soonest one out, and I'm even okay if I fly into LA and then take a bus back, but I need to leave as soon as possible."

Devon approached her carefully. "Here's what I think. It would be easiest on you if you spend the night, get some rest. The kids are going to be fine if they're going to be over at Gretchen's, and just take care of yourself. We'll take you to the airport in the morning. Let me get online and see what I can find for you and then I'll give you some choices, so just hang on a few minutes."

"You know, the kids are going to be really upset they didn't get to see you this time. I promised them when I talked to them this morning, that we would make sure they weren't away at camp when you visited. They love you and call you Aunt Kate. Did you know that?" Nick said.

"No I didn't."

"So Devon told me about your meeting with Randy. Gosh he sounds like a real mess. And she picked up some vibes about him being possibly dangerous. Did you get that at all?"

Kate had to admit that she did. And told him so.

"I guess he's a desperate man then, God I just hate to see somebody throw their whole life away. But I think that's what substance abuse does to people. It makes them crazy."

"Unfortunately, yes. Thank goodness they didn't have any kids, I guess he was married a couple of times and wouldn't that be awful if there were children involved?" Kate said.

"Amen to that. All right, so let's get the dinner together and we'll figure out what's so you go on up and get yourself showered and changed and if you need me to do any laundry, well, we could do that before you go."

"No I'm fine. Don't worry about me."

"Well, one thing's for sure, there is a devil out there, he grabs people, he shakes them around, he causes terrible things to happen. But the good news is, we don't have to fall for his tricks, Kate. I mean if you look at all of the luck and all of the things we have to feel grateful for, it's a lot more than the other way. I'm just sorry to see someone else go through so much trouble. And I hope he gets help before he starts becoming a further detriment to himself."

"I feel sorry for him too Nick. I sincerely hope that's the case as well."

In the morning, Kate was able to get a flight from Santa Rosa to the Central Valley, and then a puddle jumper direct to San Diego, which wound up adding about an extra hour to her flight time. She caught a cab, taking her home, where her car was still in the driveway. Tyler must have hitched a ride with one of his buddies because his truck was parked beside hers.

She'd gotten a message from him last night that he had arrived safe and sound. She didn't expect to hear much from him today.

She gave Gretchen a call and arranged to go pick up the girls. It was Easter vacation, their spring break, so the schools had been out for a day and would be out for the next week.

Oliver and Grady were excited to see her, little Kendall was playing with dolls at the corner, some that Gretchen still had from her brood. She walked with Angela, holding her hand, clutching a doll tightly.

"I missed you Sweetheart."

Kendall looked up at Angela, and then back at her

mother. She held the doll out to her.

"Angela says I can keep this doll. I've named her Angela. She's pretty don't you think?"

Kate took the doll in her hands and examined her. "She's beautiful, Sweetheart. She's pretty just like you are." She looked up at Angela, "Are you sure this is okay?"

Angela smirked and shook her head. "I got to get rid of some of my dolls anyway, my mom's been after me to do it. This was one of my favorites, and I think it's perfect for Kendall. Right Kendall?"

Kendall grabbed the doll, held it to her chest and nodded her head, yes.

"Okay then, let's get your things together, and where's your mom, Angela?"

"She's on the phone but she'll be right here."

When Gretchen walked in the room, it was obvious she'd been crying. "God damned men!" she sniffled.

"What is it?"

"Well, that big lump of a husband of mine, he told me he was going to take them to the airport? He did, but then he fucking got on the plane too. I just talked to him. I am so pissed at him."

"Don't worry about it, Gretchen, Trace will be fine. He wants to go. He also knows Portland better than some of the others, I think."

"Yes, you did ask me about him and I did say that

he'd be willing to go but damn I didn't think he'd do that. Now we're all alone here. Do you want to just stay here at my place and we can all be together? I mean I hate to have you be at your house without a man and me be at my house without a man. Why don't we just all stay here for a few days until they come back?"

Kate thought about it and it actually sounded pretty good.

"I'll have to go back to the house to get more of their clothes, some for me, but that should work."

"Cool deal. We can stay up all night and watch romance movies."

They both laughed. It was exactly what Kate needed this evening. She needed her kids, and she needed her sister.

"On one condition, Gretchen."

"What's that?"

"You let me buy delivery tonight. I'm starved for pizza," Kate said.

All the kids, including Angela, jumped for joy.

CHAPTER 17

"**Y**OUR MARRIAGE GOING to survive this, Trace?" Tyler asked his buddy. They were traveling in Fredo's truck toward the military transport hangar.

"I think so, she's in tears. I'm glad that Kate's with her. It's tough but she has to understand. I mean, you're my fucking brother-in-law. You think I'm going to let you go through all this crap by yourself? These are your parents for Christ's sakes."

"Oh Trace," said Fredo. "You better be careful with that my friend. I hope you smoothed it over pretty good. Otherwise, you may be sleeping on the couch, and that's one step toward divorce."

Danny laughed. "You probably should listen to Fredo, Trace. He knows whereof he speaks."

"Listen to you fuckhead?" said Tyler. He wanted to draw them into focusing on the mission at hand.

"Okay, we've got a whole lot of things to strategize, and you guys are worried about getting laid? So let's just cut it out and let's pay attention to completing the mission without any major sacrifice."

Trace leaned in and pointed to Tyler with his thumb as if hitchhiking. "He says he's going to quit the Teams, but I think he's going for Kyle's job don't you think?"

The rest of the guys spent the next few minutes giving their highly valued opinion about that.

The transport plane they picked up was a sheer bucket of bolts. It had something wrong with one of its stabilizers, so the darn thing listed a little bit to the left, which was not going to be acceptable if they were delivering high-valued equipment, but for a bunch of raspy old SEALs, it would be fine. There was something perfect about taking the most antiquated behemoth of a ship they could take. *As long as it gets us there*, Tyler thought to himself.

They landed in the private military airport, which was just adjacent to the private airport outside of Portland. There, a military Jeep was waiting for them to escort them out of the field. Though they were all active duty, they didn't have clearance to actually use the site, so they needed to be escorted away, and it would be reported that they had been delivered on time.

There was an old Suburban left for them to use, something that Bryce had arranged. He was to meet them at Riley's compound, and he promised them he'd have some beers and some food for them.

Tyler was anxious to get the updates.

"Hey Tyler, I did bring some fire power. I know we're not supposed to, but I did anyway. Is that going to be cool or do I have to leave that behind at Riley's place?"

"God I don't care. I'm going to let Bryce answer that one. But I will tell you the gun laws here in Oregon are just super strict. You're going to have to be careful about that. No open carry, and as far as the concealed carry, well if they don't know about it, you just don't want to get caught."

"And I have the same question with some of my explosive devices. I know that's why you asked me to come along, so I packed a nice little wad of charges that might come in handy. Do we have any idea where they are? What kind of building they're housed in?"

"No, gents, we don't even know that they've been kidnapped. They could have fallen down in the supermarket and helping each other get up the other one fell down and they could be in the hospital for all I know, but that's just not how it's playing out. So we're going to treat it like it's a regular hostage situation kidnapping. And that's what the Bone Frog group does so well. That's why I asked them."

They drove through downtown Portland and Tyler

veered off to the side and took them down through the warehouse district just as it was turning dusk. He didn't want to be down there in an old Suburban with just men in the car, which could flame some kind of gang activity. But he pointed to the strip of charred earth that extended down several blocks, and the big crater behind the Grays' warehouse where the paint manufacturer blew up.

"Was this an intentional set-off or did it just combust?" asked Fredo.

"We're thinking it was just a coincidence, it got hot, and it just combusted. I'm not sure anybody has said anything about explosives, and so far there haven't been any rounds fired either, but somebody did paint this substance and that is highly flammable. But it doesn't explode."

"Sure I've heard of that. It's called boat paste. Originally used to burn barnacles off ships' bottoms. They also use that shit when they want to ram something and cause further destruction. They used to use it in Vietnam believe it or not on some of those little rubber boats. You paste that stuff on the front of it, it hits a tree and just goes up like nobody's business," said Fredo.

"It's funny I've never seen it before. But the fire marshal knew all about it. It's a derivative of some kind and we have some refineries nearby, but he thinks somebody might have picked it up during the disposal period, because that stuff he said isn't used as much as it's dumped. They take it to the Superfund site."

They veered to the left and skirting down along the banks of the Columbia River drove past ten or twelve train track lines, passed the station and large storage yard, and then turned left to head west, and began to climb several hills, winding back and forth until they got to the top.

Tyler showed them his parents' home. "I got keys to it, so we can just do a quick run through here, I don't want to spend very much time because I don't want anybody to know that we've been here. Just do a quick run through, we can do it better in the daylight. I don't want to turn on any lights tonight."

They spread out over the house, everybody searching individual things, of course the first thing several of them looked for was any arms, and Tyler confirmed that his mom and dad didn't own any. There were valuable items that were still left in the house, so it didn't appear to be a robbery of some kind. Mrs. Gray even had her wedding rings in a little ceramic dish by the side of the sink in the master bathroom.

Tyler knew his father kept a safe with some important documents in it, and he found it to be intact in his father's side of the closet, behind the shoe shelves. Nothing appeared to be touched but he didn't have the combination.

Trace brought some baggies to pick up little bits and pieces of things. He pointed to the cell phones that were still charging, and Tyler nodded that yes, he should take them both. He also instructed him to take the charging cords since somebody would have used their thumbprint to get it attached to the wall, and it might make for some good evidence.

"What are we going to do if the police say they don't have it, when they come back and it's gone?"

"I think there are so many cooks in the stew—there's FBI and the local police, even the county sheriff, fire department, the fire inspector—they're probably just going to figure that somebody else picked it up and bagged it. We're not going to touch it. We're just going to see if there's anything of interest on it. I don't think I have any of my mom's passcodes, but I'm going to look through my list just in case. And the biggest thing is going to be who's leaving the messages right now. I want to know who they are."

"Roger that," said Trace.

The four SEALs piled into the Suburban, holding the few items they'd taken from the house in a paper lunch bag. Fredo stowed it underneath the second seat and placed an old blanket in front of it to hide it from view. Within ten minutes, they were driving through the metal gate of Colin Riley's castle on the hill. The gate opened as they approached it, and Tyler drove through very slowly, coming to a halt near the front door entrance.

"Would you look at that?" said Danny.

The lights were stunning from the top of the hill, and the air was so fresh and free of pollutants from all of the rains and the winds that Portland got, the stars appeared to be extra bright this evening. It was a pretty awesome sight.

"Wait till you see the inside of the house, guys. I mean if you think this looks like a castle now, just wait till you see it."

An interesting landscape display was in the garden area just before the front door. There had been pots and trees planted in pots that had been tipped over and cracked and made to look like some kind of a Roman ruin. Flowers draped over all these broken pieces, and to the side, without the aid of any protection, was Colin Riley's old wheelchair. Someone had cut out the seat of the chair in a circle, and placed a wandering petunia plant there, which took over part of the back and one side of the arm. It was a very touching and fitting memorial to a man who lived larger than his body was capable of carrying him. He spawned the organization, having lost his son to a drug overdose and almost losing a daughter as well. The SEALs were responsible for returning her to him. He lived a brief period of time after the rescue and died a happy man knowing that his legacy would be continued and that some of the very SEALs who had rescued his daughter would be joining his team.

Before Tyler could get to the front door, Bryce Tanner and several other men came barreling out of the house. He could see in the distance several huge flat screen TVs, one of them with a basketball game playing.

"Hey, Tyler! Welcome, Brother. And all of you guys, I know I met you, Trace. I've met you, Danny, I think, but I haven't met you before, have I?" He looked at Fredo.

"I think if you had met me you would remember me. I sure as hell have never seen this place before. Nice digs."

"Well, this belonged to Mr. Riley, of course, and he left this as a training ground, dorm, strategy session think tank, if you will. He left this for all of us to use for as long as we keep the business going. It's been nice to have one place to congregate."

"Are Jenna and Kelly about?" asked Trace.

"Jenna should be here tomorrow. I'm not sure who else is going to be dropping by. Sven Tolar is back in Norway right now, dealing with a family matter."

As soon as they got inside, Bryce showed the men their rooms and let them select the sleeping arrangements. And he also showed them the equipment they had, where they could store any equipment they brought, explained to them they could help themselves to any of the food in the kitchen, and advised that no business was ever talked when the house was being cleaned or the food was being prepared by outside chefs. Then he began the process of updating everyone as to what he'd discovered.

"I found out this Gregory Poplin character is the product of two radical hippies, who got involved in protests during the civil rights movement in the sixties and seventies and wound up going to prison for blowing up a Bank of America building down in Silicon Valley years ago. I guess Gregory Poplin was a child of three at the time, so he was raised by his aunt, his mother's sister. Both of his parents have since passed on, his father in a prison riot and his mother of cancer in prison. He has always been an advocate for lawlessness and lack of police protection; he's an anarchist. A very dangerous one, because he has collected a large war chest of many millions of dollars. It's part of the shadowy underworld of donations that come in and don't get reported, that swing elections. They're bad people. I'm all for making the prison system humane, fair, honest, clean, and danger-free. I'm not for attacking police and fire and burning down buildings and ruining people's lives and their livelihood. This gentleman doesn't seem to quite know the difference between the two."

"So he got this woman out of prison then, correct?" asked Danny.

"Yes, he did. And if I'm not mistaken, there may be some kind of a romance going between the two of them. This is just a rumor. She seems to spend quite a bit of time in his penthouse apartment. And, oh yes, this is the rich part. He claims he is out to support the people, but it's only known to a handful of people that he owns a very fancy $5 million apartment that's roughly 3,500 square feet at the top of one of the insurance buildings downtown. He can see firsthand every single riot and what it does to the downtown area. With binoculars, I'm sure he could have watched the warehouses burn. There are a lot of politicians, especially small local ones, assistant DAs, school board members, people who don't have a lot of political clout, there's a lot of people afraid of him. And they should be."

"Bryce, so you say Sheila was seen going in and out of his place?"

"We've had somebody over at the building ever since your phone call, Tyler. She is a regular visitor, and she frequently spends the night. That's why I believe there is a romantic connection. She is quite a bit younger than he is, but you know how that goes."

"What about my parents?" Tyler asked.

"We're still working on that. I'm trying to get some more information from the inspector's office, but they've all of a sudden gotten pretty tightlipped. I have a feeling they are onto something, and they just don't want to share it. Were you able to pick up their phones?" he asked Tyler.

"Yes, sir, we have them right here." Tyler spread the phones in their baggies on the counter in the kitchen.

"Ronnie?" He called to the other room.

A young boy with frizzy brown hair and huge thick horn-rimmed glasses came running in. He didn't look like he was more than fourteen or fifteen years old, but Tyler recognized him as being one of the sons of one of the Marines who had joined the team. "Okay. This is Ronnie, and he's our electronic specialist. There isn't anything he can't hack or get into. He's going to take these phones and try to get a pattern of where they were up until the time they were plugged in. If my hunch is correct, they may have picked up whoever it was that located them at a store of some kind, perhaps shopping or having a lunch downtown. My feeling is they were recognized, followed, and then they were abducted. As far as we know, there is no ransom demand and no statements have been given to the paper."

"Does the FBI believe they are kidnapped or does the FBI believe they have been killed?" asked Tyler. His comment brought a hush over the group. Tyler, realizing he'd suddenly shut down all conversation, gave his justification, "Hey, I want to know what everybody thinks. I need to know going in what their approach is. If they think my parents are dead, I want to know that. And I want to know why they think that, because that's a clue."

Bryce nodded his head. "Actually, Tyler that's a very good point. I know from my years on the force, if it is believed that the hostage is alive, there's a lot greater care taken to not be discovered. If it's a question of where the bodies are, then it's a full-scale snatch and grab. They go out and they snag everybody they can, they ask as many questions as they can, and hope that they've found somebody that has some kind of knowledge of it. So far, we think that they're assuming that your parents are still alive. But they don't know where they are or who took them."

"Ronnie, I want you to trace where these phones have been, where these phones have gone, and give me a physical map of the Portland area where they traveled to at what time of the day, okay?"

"You got it, sir," said Ronnie. He grabbed the bags and disappeared.

"Just so you know, the police are probably tracing

this as well. They have the benefit of having a cell tower to get information from. We're getting it from the source. They don't really physically need the phones to get that information, whereas this is the only way we could get it. The one thing they don't get clearly is messages, people that called and left a message on their phone. That's what we're also going to look at."

Bryce made mention that the men could help themselves to sandwiches in the refrigerator. He suggested everyone shower, get ready for bed, and that first thing in the morning, at daybreak, they would resume their activities.

"That should give Ronnie enough time to get all the data out of these phones, and if any of you get any messages or calls from anybody else on the outside, if it has to do with this investigation, I want you to let me know about it. There's going to be some people that'll snoop around innocently trying to find out what we're doing. They may not all be innocent participants."

"Any other questions?"

Tyler spoke up next. "Bryce, I want to thank you. I want to thank all of you for doing your jobs here. And, Trace, I'm sorry about your marriage."

Everybody chuckled.

"It means a lot to me that you're here. If at any time you guys have to leave, don't feel like you have to stay. This is a non-paid situation, and Bryce has been kind enough to donate his buildings and his services, so there is no burden financially on me or on my parents' estate. That said, I want you to clean up after yourselves, cook for yourselves, and don't be a burden to everybody else. You're going to meet the rest of the team in the morning, and I think you'll find them a real solid group of guys. Except for a couple of people you will be the only other ones staying at this house. Everyone else lives off campus. But for this particular operation I'm going to have all of you stay here, even I won't be going and staying in my parents' house. If anybody comes to the house, Bryce is the only one that answers the door. Are we clear about that?" Everybody nodded their heads.

"Once again guys, get some rest, and let's kick it in gear tomorrow."

CHAPTER 18

I N THE MORNING over coffee, the men sat, laid out all of the places they needed to cover, and the timing of it.

"How you want to do this, Tyler?" asked Bryce. "You want to be lead on this? Or you want us to assign and be point?"

"My ego isn't attached. I want to do whatever's going to get them out safe. I'd say our mission is first to verify that they're there where they are, who's guarding them, and then who's going to stand by and make sure the attorney and Sheila are detained so that the authorities can grab them."

"Sounds good to me. Anyone with questions so far?"

"Let's hear the plan," said Danny.

"Let me begin," Tyler said, "by saying we don't want any loss of life, on either side. We want to incapacitate not kill." Tyler looked at the eyes of the team around him. "I know I don't have to say that, and you guys will be appropriate. But I also don't want any of you harmed, so the use of lethal force is only necessary if it's going to save the lives of one of our team or one of the hostages." He shrugged his shoulders. "That's how I am and I think Bryce you can take it from there."

"Okay. Good reminder of the rules of engagement. So it's going to be a standard cover all the points operation, we follow and identify all the moving parts so we don't encounter any unexpected consequences. I got two men downtown in front of the attorney's building, and I've got one guy up on the floor. We'll be getting good intel about whether or not the attorney and Sheila have left the building. We assume there will be others there, but whoever comes out of that building this morning, we're going to follow. All of them."

Bryce laid out the teams in twos, indicating that each moving part would have coverage of some kind, and that once the holding location for Tyler's parents was identified, they would be verifying proof of life first, and second of all how much manpower they were going to need to conduct the rescue. All in all, they had ten men present and another five out in the field.

Ronnie had identified locations used the day before the Grays went missing, through their cell phones. He was invited to explain and show on the map where they went that day.

"It looks like they went shopping at a supermarket here and they went down to a bookstore in this area here. I believe this is Powell's. Then they bypassed the area where the demonstrations were, and several blocks to the west they stopped at an art supply store, where we believe they purchased some items. They were there for quite a while, almost forty-five minutes."

"That sounds like them," said Tyler. "My mom probably wants to paint. She does that when she gets nervous. She probably went to the arts supply store to buy something."

"OK, good. One of two things happened, either their house was being watched and they were tailed the whole time, or they picked up somebody at the supply shop, at the grocery store or at Powell's. My money's on the fact that they were monitored from the minute they stepped out of the house," said Bryce.

"So how does that jive with the appearance and disappearance of the van? The witness from the neighborhood who saw it come and go?" asked Tyler.

"I believe they came back and then were forced to leave, and someone went back to get something. Perhaps some clothes, perhaps some medication. Something."

"My dad's on quite a bit of medication and takes about six pills every day," said Tyler.

"So that would explain it then, they were told

where to come in and where to get the medication, and that shows to me," Bryce barked, "they intended to keep them alive. Or at least for a period of time. I'm not quite sure what the overall game plan was but at least for managing their health, they needed to go back and get his meds. So that would make total sense to me," said Bryce.

"Do you suppose they would be housed in the penthouse?" asked Trace.

"We've been monitoring the penthouse for several days now, and there has been no indication that either of his parents are there. But there have been people coming and going, probably members of Mr. Poplin's inner circle. I don't think he'd be so stupid as to keep them there, because it would implicate him. He's smarter than that."

Tyler agreed with Bryce's opinion. Unfortunately, he didn't like the waiting part.

"So how do we arrange ourselves? Where do we wait? Staying here is too far away," he said.

"I think they would stay pretty close to the downtown area. I'm going to guess and again it's just a guess, that they want to stay mobile, they want to stay in an area where they feel comfortable, and the downtown area that has been taken over, is good cover for them. I mean some of his team could even be sleeping in tents down with the homeless encampments. It would be very hard to find them in that crowd. Also, they wouldn't stand out as being police or military or the good guys, and I think the homeless people would give them cover willingly."

"So, with three at the penthouse, and two or three at my parents' house, where are you going to want us stationed?" asked Tyler.

Bryce showed certain corners where they could have access to buildings, they also suggested that people stay in vehicles where they could be kept warm, and if they needed to move quickly they would have wheels. "This is his home," he said as he pointed to the location of the penthouse building. "And this is his office one block away. Somewhere between there is where I need the rest of you located. We need to cover anybody at any time moving between those two places."

"If you want any fire cover, I'm going to need some kind of a building with windows that open so I can do that for you guys," said Danny. "Any suggestions, Bryce?"

Bryce pointed to a building four doors down from the lawyer's office building. "This has a balcony on the fifth floor with a cafe that sometimes is open there. That would be a good place because it has a slatted railing, and you could see through if you were belly on the ground. It also has a good vantage point to several areas. However, you'd have to avoid being observed from the top of the penthouse which is directly perpendicular to this building. So, this area and this area." He demonstrated with his finger. "These areas would be visible. You'd want to avoid them. I would go there Danny."

"Roger that. And who do I take?"

"I want a volunteer."

One of Bryce's men raised his hand. "Okay. You two take one of our trucks and go make it down there. And please inform me when you're in place. And Connor," he addressed his man, "The security guard at the bottom of this building is a friend of ours, all you have to do is show your card and explain that there's a surveillance detail that we want to do from the rooftop. He'll be cooperative."

"Roger that." Danny and Connor left the room.

"Okay. That leaves these teams," and he demonstrated who was going where. "Tyler, I'd like you to stay with me. Trace, you and Fredo to stay together. But make sure you stay in radio communication with your Invisios, Fredo, if we need some firepower, I'm going to ask you to bring a small pack."

"You got it, sir," said Fredo.

"Nothing too flashy, just something that would get attention or bust open a door if we need it. This time of the morning, a lot of the downtown is going to be just completely dead. There will be some big trucks making deliveries, there will be janitorial services finishing up, it's busy from a commercial side of things but inside the offices, most of them except for the stock brokerages, will be completely empty. It'll be a good opportunity for us to get embedded."

Everyone agreed they understood where they were going and left in pairs.

On the way downtown to their vantage point, Tyler needed Bryce to answer a couple of questions. "You've been here, what? Three, four years now, Bryce?"

"Yes sir. About four years now. We moved the whole family here about six months after I started, just trying to make sure that it was going to be a good fit."

"So how do they feel about this now with all the stuff going on downtown?"

"Well I don't have to tell you that it's good for business, we have done a lot of little jobs just protecting bank presidents and CEOs coming in to attend board meetings and things of that nature, with the climate being the way it is. The police really have their hands full and with the numbers of cutbacks that have gone on and their hesitancy to stir things up, they really can't be counted on for protection. So we've been really busy with these small jobs."

"But you didn't answer my question."

Bryce turned down one of the main streets leading

toward the bookstore, heading right through the center of the free zone where there were barricades, posters and even occasionally armed protestors manning the perimeter, dressed in full body armor.

"What does that remind you of?"

"Fuckin' A. You name the city. Djibouti, Ngala, Cape City."

"I'm not going to lie to you and say that my wife loves it here. It's probably not safe for her to live anywhere else though. I don't want to have to defend her from a long distance. So in order to take this position over and run this team, it was important that she move here. If she didn't want to willingly, then no way was I going to take the job. Since then, that's been the biggest problem in recruiting. I can't get them to come. The guys want to, but the families don't want to live here anymore. At first, it was just a nuisance. Now it's a real health and safety issue. There's so many companies leaving that the condition of the downtown is not going to improve. It's just going to get worse and worse. Not until they start voting in some people that want to do something about it. So that's where we're at."

"Sounds like the perfect profile for your team is experienced older guy, divorced, with grown kids. Doesn't have a family to protect, right?"

"That's about right. You probably know that's the

biggest attrition for SEALs—the families they leave behind. Takes a special guy to do what you guys do and have loved ones at home. Changes your perspective real fast, doesn't it?"

"Is that why you left Team 5?"

"Yup. My wife thought it would be safer to go work for SDPD. How about that decision? Couldn't even protect my little girl."

Tyler didn't want to pry. Bryce had told him a lot right there.

"No regrets. My wife and I are as tight as we've been. She knows I love this work. And we have an axe to grind with the bad guys."

"Are you glad you did it?"

"I am, my daughter was so severely traumatized with the kidnapping and attempted slavery caper, she is still going through therapy four and a half years later. No kid should have to go through that. If I can save somebody else from having to experience that level of violence for their kids, I want to do it. And I wouldn't do it if I didn't have the support of my family. She sees things in school still that just makes my wife and I shake our heads. I just don't understand why we don't protect our kids anymore."

"Word there, Bryce."

"Why did we decide to turn on them, quit supporting them, quit keeping them safe? When did that happen? When did that become an American thing? I will never ever accept that. And if I have to fight the rest of my life to see to it that people who just want to live, go to work, and be safe... If I spend the rest of my life doing that, it's good work. And in a way, it's better work than police work. We have resources and assets and information, most of the departments are cooperative with us. And we soon learn where the stumbling blocks are, so we have cooperation because people in the police and rescue communities know we're trying to do good. We're trying to make their job easier. I think it's worth it."

"You know Bryce, if things don't improve, I can see us facing someday the fact that our inner cities and our societies are torn apart by some of these people, trying to destroy the fabric of the family and everything we hold dear, you may find that it's even more challenging more dangerous than what we did overseas."

"No doubt, Tyler I think you're right. Overseas we had the brotherhood, we had the team behind us, we had guys on either side of us that were willing to die for us. Here when you're in a backup position, you're working with people who didn't sign on for that. They want to go home to their families too and they aren't in it to solve the problem, they're in it to manage the problem for now. Not their fault. It's just set up wrong. Their hands are tied. Maybe someday that's going to be us overseas too I don't know. I just hope that we all remember that famous quote."

"Which one?"

"Evil exists when good men do nothing."

Tyler nodded his head. He knew now, even before their little mission began, that this was not going to be the hill he wanted to die on. There were other things he was being called to do. He couldn't ask Kate or Oliver and Grady or Kendall to be exposed to all this. He just could never do it.

Once they were in place the check-ins began. Movement was noted, pictures were being transmitted to cell phones, there was still no trace of the attorney or Sheila, but several of Mr. Poplin's staff were seen going back and forth between his residence and the office. A van left the office building and two teams followed carefully at a safe distance behind. It headed down toward the railroad tracks and the warehouse district, and pulled into an old packing plant, with a chain link fence all around the perimeter. The fence was guarded with two armed guards, opened for the van to be let in, and then closed behind them. Three men got out of the van with boxes, and went inside.

Pictures were sent to Tyler and Bryce.

"That's going to be my pick. Bryce I think they're there. It's just a hunch I have."

"The fact they went from Poplin's office to this

warehouse, does point to that doesn't it?"

They phoned in to Bryce's office the license plate of the van, and it was registered to a nonprofit that assisted homeless. It didn't appear that the building housed homeless population, at least there wasn't a license registered to do so, which was city-required.

Two other teams followed other individuals who blended into the crowd downtown, some were passing out food stuffs, others were passing out blankets. They appeared to be homeless paid staffers, and could have been messengers used to distribute money and communication to other teams that could be down on the ground in the tents. Tyler and Bryce stayed put, until the sun had fully risen, and people started arriving at work. The city's population expanded to double what it was before dawn.

The team watching the warehouse was ordered to put up a drone, and to see if they could get some kind of video of what was located inside the building. As the footage came in to Bryce's computer, he and Tyler watched as they saw a large area set up with tables and piles of food stuffs and blankets and water bottles and other things related to the homeless crisis. There also was a portion of the downstairs set-up as a meeting room with metal chairs in rows facing a small dais in front. There were several offices that were at the far side of the building, facing the wharf, where the drapes were pulled and there was no interior light. While the drone was shooting the footage, one of the doors opened revealing a small lighted cubicle and, on the floor, several mattresses. Tyler looked closely at the mattresses in front of him on the screen and recognized the long gray hair of his mother.

"That's her. She's there. Is she alive?" He asked.

"I'm fairly sure if she wasn't, they wouldn't keep her here," said Bryce.

The drone was instructed to move around the building one more rotation, and then attempt to find a window on the outside that might have access to this office. From the outside they could see about ten feet up was the height of the window. It was going to require a ladder or scaling tools to get a man or two up in there. But the drone could only see through parts of it, as the blinds were twisted and crooked, and only revealed part of the room. But there was no mistaking the fact that Tyler's mother and probably father were moving. They were in sleeping position and rolling from side to side occasionally.

"Well, that's a sign of life then. That's a go for us." Bryce whispered commands to several others on the team.

Tyler thought in his heart thank God.

The rest of the teams were alerted, several were pulled off the downtown surveillance and switched over to the warehouse district. There were six, two that would scale the fence and cut the electrical power, two more that were going to be ramming the fence with their truck, and coming from the back of the truck two more to run in and face any opposition they'd find in the building. Other than the one person that moved in and out of the office, the building didn't appear to be very well guarded.

Tyler and Bryce moved positions just as the six-man team went forward. Within a minute, the gate was disabled, both of the guards were restrained and given a tranquilizer, the two-man team who scaled the wire fencing, successfully cut the electrical power to the entire area, and managed to go in through the main door. Scanning for any additional guards inside. They found two near a makeshift kitchen, crept up on them and disabled them, giving them a nice sleepy-time dose. They marked their location and confirmed it was clear.

"Don't see any gremlins, gents," they heard Danny say over his Invisio.

"You want to go in Tyler? I don't think we've got any resistance right now. Unless somebody's watching the site."

"Hell yeah. I'd like me to be the one my mom sees first."

They were alerted to an additional van headed their

way from the office building. A team was re-routed, and the van was detained several blocks before being able to see the warehouse site. The driver was detained, disarmed, zip tied, and tranquilized. The second passenger met the same fate. In the back of the vehicle, they found containers of gasoline, rags and material for making Molotov cocktails. They took pictures and sent word to their police liaison what they'd discovered and where they could come find the van. This would also give them additional backup in case things didn't go well inside the building. The police would be close.

Tyler and Bryce walked through the open gateway, crossed the gravel yard and into the building. It was eerie and cold, drafty. But silent. Tyler ran to the door he'd seen on the drone footage, opened it while Bryce covered him from behind and then above his head. He used his gun light, with no electricity in the building.

Tyler called out. "Mom? It's me."

He could hear rustling in the corner and then her faint voice, "Oh my God Tyler you're here. I knew you'd come. We're okay. We're scared to death but we're okay. Your dad's not doing very well right now but now that you're here, we're okay."

CHAPTER 19

K ATE GOT THE call at around ten in the morning.

"They're safe, Sweetheart. As soon as I can, I'm coming home."

"Thank you for letting me know. Are you okay?" she asked.

"I'm much better now."

"Was it that group that was holding them? Were they in fact kidnapped?"

"Yes, they were. And hopefully, we got them all. We've got Sheila, and we found her attorney there too. The police have detained them, but they're not likely to be able to hold them. At least they were found. And a whole bunch of the attorney's staff were found implicated, and there's going to be a huge investigation of this. I'm not sure it's going to make much difference, but for now, his network, his gang is a little bit out of action."

"Of course he is. I would not have expected it any

differently. I'm so glad that you went up there, but I'm going to be so much happier when you get back here. I've been doing a lot of thinking, Tyler. A whole lot of thinking."

"Me too, Sweetheart. But I just wanted you to know I'm coming home. I'll text you when I get a flight out of here."

Gretchen was sitting up in bed, waiting to hear confirmation that everybody was safe.

"Did he say anything about Trace?"

"All he said was everybody's safe. I'm sure he'll call, Gretchen. Don't worry."

"I hate it when we fight before he goes off and does something. I just feel like a complete heel. You would think I could just watch my mouth and not say some of the things I say. And he does it too, so I'm going to work on that," she said.

"It's all good, Gretchen. If you didn't care so much, it wouldn't bother you at all. But he just did something heroic this morning, and I know you're going to celebrate it. And whatever happened before he left, I'm sure he didn't mean to offend you or make you angry."

"But he promised me he was just going to drop them off."

"Yeah, and then he looked at his buddies, and he saw them, and he decided, hey, they're going to put their life on the line to go rescue somebody and why the hell can't I go too? And he just did it. And he's also family with us being sisters. He's family. He's doing it for you. He's doing it for me. He's doing it for all our kids."

"You're right. You're right. I guess I better call Mom."

"Yes, please do. And would you also tell her that it looks like they've found and captured Sheila?"

"Will do."

Kate went downstairs and began preparing coffee for her and Gretchen. While she was waiting for the water to boil, she called Devon.

"Oh, I've been thinking about you guys. Is everything okay?"

"Yeah, they went up there. They found Tyler's parents. They used the Bone Frog Group and a couple of the guys went from Team 3, but they got it done. They found everybody, and nobody got hurt. They found Sheila, too, and her attorney-boyfriend, I guess."

"That's wonderful. Oh, I'm so relieved, Kate. You must be too."

"I am. I just want to see him. I just want to physically see him and hug him."

"I understand completely. Listen, I won't take more of your time. You just tell him we're proud of him. I will let Nick know. He's going to be thrilled. And when you're ready, let's plan that trip. I want you guys to come up and spend just a few days with us. No talk about business or wineries or anything. Just come for vacation. You need it."

"You know, Devon, that's probably the wisest piece of advice you've ever given me. And I think the answer on that's going to be yes. But of course, I got to check with the boss."

"Yes, you do. Yes, you do. Thanks for letting me know."

She finished the coffee, and one by one, the kids started getting up, and the TV went on before permission was given. Gretchen walked past the big screen, rolling her eyes but making her way to the kitchen. She looked like a zombie, her arms outstretched and grabbing the coffee cup. She pulled the whipping cream from the refrigerator, poured nearly a quarter cup of cream into her Happy Mother's Day mug, and then guzzled half of it down before she got the refrigerator door closed.

"Okay, so now I'm going to be normal. Thank God I had my first sip of coffee."

Kate set her mug down and walked over to Gretchen, the two sisters hugging each other in front of the refrigerator door, still open.

"Thank you so much for your strength, Gretchen. Thank you for letting me stay here. Looks like we're going to be leaving sooner than I thought."

Carefully, Kate moved her sister away and closed the refrigerator door behind her. She took Gretchen's hand and brought her into the dining room table, where they sat.

"I can't wait for them to get home, Kate."

"I hate this part. I don't do waiting very well, Sis."

"That's what Trace says all the time."

"So does Tyler!"

TYLER CAME HOME about five hours later. He'd texted Kate, and she informed him that she and the kids were back home, waiting for him.

The sight of him at the door instantly had her heart fluttering and her knees wobbling. It was always like that for her. That first sighting, the first time they looked at each other after they'd been gone even for short periods of time. But especially if there was danger involved, some kind of an op or a training. It was so sweet to have him back. She ran to him, and he dropped his duty bag, grabbing her by the waist and planting a big kiss on her lips.

"As I said before, it's worth it to go away for the welcome I get when I'm home." He smiled, and she buried her head underneath this chin.

"Thank you, Tyler, for doing that for your folks. I'm sure you wanted to stay with them longer, but thank you for coming home."

"Well, they're going to be fine. They admitted them both to the hospital, and they're going to do a full check on both of them to make sure they didn't get exposed to something. They didn't eat very much, and he was off his meds for a day, but they're in the same hospital room, I'm sure driving the nurses crazy."

"Probably teaching painting lessons."

Tyler chuckled. "I wouldn't be surprised…"

"Any idea what's happening with the insurance, and have they made any plans about rebuilding?"

"I think I'm going to let my mom talk to you about that."

"What do you mean?"

"Oh, that's her story to tell. She'll get around to it. She wants to do it her way. I want her to have the opportunity to do it. I just want to be home. I don't want to talk about insurances or anything. I just want to be home."

"Well, the kids are out back. They'd love to see you."

"I'll do that, and then I'd like to take a nice long shower with my girl. If she'll have me?"

"I would love nothing better, my love."

She knew he was probably dead tired, the adrenalin of the op having worn off with inactivity. He was either on full tilt or off. There wasn't any in-between. Still, he ran outside and greeted his kids and didn't show a speck of the fatigue she knew he was feeling. It was what he did and did so well.

In the next few days, Tyler and Kate jumped into their old routine. The boys were climbing all over Tyler whenever he sat down. Kendall asked him to read stories to her, and they took a small trip to a Lego store and purchased a big space shuttle model that was going to take them the better part of a week to put together. The boys were rapidly spilling all the pieces all over the floor, and Kate knew they'd be lucky to get it put together without missing parts showing. But it was fun watching them play, seeing Tyler patiently work with his boys. His boys were just like him, she thought. Exuberant, full of energy, curious, and bright. It was like three little boys working on that space shuttle rather than a father and two sons. It warmed her heart just watching them.

Kendall had been extra cuddly and extremely motherly with her doll. But after the first few days, the newness of the doll wore off, and it was relegated to several of her other stuffed toys. She had a small zoo: a stuffed dinosaur, a pig, a snake, and a big red rooster with a floppy top knot. The doll sat right in the middle of the jungle team, looking like she ran the place.

Kate started working with Kendall on drawing pictures between the lines, doing fine motor skill type activities. She even bought a set of special markers and scissors so she could make her own stickers. And for several days, the boys had little stickers on their butts or on the back of their shirts, little reminders of sunflowers and smiley faces all over the bathroom mirror and even on the shower curtain.

They went to the farmers' market and picked out colorful eggs. Someone was there selling green and brown and purple eggs, which delighted the kids completely. Kate thought of Devon and Nick's chickens. She thought of Zak and Amy's farm and her chickens and her vegetable garden. Kate decided that even though their lot size was small, it was large compared to the rest of the neighborhood. She'd try her hand at doing some vegetables herself.

The next day, she and Kendall laid out an area with the small hoe she bought that was Kendall's size. She had her make divots in the soil and then helped her plant peas, which were large enough for her little fingers to carry. Of course, she didn't plant them evenly, and Kate left them just the way they were done. They covered the peas over with planting mix soil and then watered it down.

It turned out to be one of Kendall's favorite jobs, to water and then accidentally spray her mother as well.

About five days after Tyler returned, the Team started their workout for their next rotation in Mexico. And then one day, when he was off with the team, she got a call from his mother.

"Kate, this is Deidre."

"Hi, Mom. How are you doing?"

"Oh, I'm fine, my heart and my liver and all my vital organs are those of a forty-year-old, they tell me. So I guess I'm going to live to be a hundred and something."

"Well, that's good news. How about Dad?"

"It's a little more complicated for him, but they're adjusting some of his medication, and they're hoping they can get rid of the cramping he's getting probably from the hypertension pills. But they'll get it straight. He's also gotten a clean bill of health. So we're grateful."

"I love hearing this. You gave us quite a scare, and I'm so sorry you had to go through all that."

"Well, the way I look at it, Kate, it's just like what I thought after the fire, and you said it as well, God just wanted me to lighten up and maybe change what I was doing. I missed my painting, but I've started getting back into it. Larry doesn't like the smell, but we'll fix that in time. I think now that the people who did this have been caught, hopefully they'll be incarcerated, and in a way, it's safer here than it was before."

Kate inhaled and held her breath. She really didn't want to hear what she feared her mother-in-law was going to say. "Well, I think it's a good wake up call for all of us to pay attention to what's going on around us, and hopefully, we've learned some lessons, and we'll put into place some things that will keep us all safer. I'm going to try to look at the positive side of things. But I am also very glad that those who went after you guys will be punished. And I hope they make it stick."

"Larry and I have talked, and we are thinking about what we'd like to do. I think one of the things I miss most is being close to my grandchildren. Being close to you and Tyler. And I can't ask you guys to move up here, so Larry and I have decided that we will put the house on the market and maybe use the funds to buy something down there. You know, they gave us an unbelievable offer. I think with the abduction happening, they threw in more than they'd planned on doing, not that they had to. They should have settled before! Who would have thought that would happen?"

Kate chuckled, glad to hear the happiness in her voice.

"Now Devon has told me, because I had her help me find a good realtor locally here, that you were looking for spaces in Santa Rosa."

"Well, that was before, I think we're going to stay put now. I think we need to stay here until the kids are done with school."

"Well, that's good, because that's what I want too. And I've been thinking we could still do a wedding center, except it would be different than the other ones. It would be filled with artwork and big stained glass windows, a big building with beautiful sunlight coming in from all directions, and maybe it would be the type of place that would be sort of eclectic and different. Close to the beach perhaps? It'd be lovely if we could make some beautiful gardens around it. And we could display artists' paintings and sculptures. We could have gallery events for local artists, benefits for the arts community. But most importantly, we could use it as a wedding center and a catering office for you."

Kate was shocked. "Are you serious?"

"Of course I'm serious, Dear. I want to propose that you and I become partners. Not Tyler and Larry and you and I, just you and I. I'd like to be your partner. And if your sister Gretchen is interested or the girls want to be involved, I'd be in favor of that too. I just think we should work together and make those dreams that you had about creating a beautiful place to gather in, that we could make that happen in San Diego. I think we'd still have enough to buy a little house, not the size house we have now, but something comfortable, perhaps near your place."

"Are you sure? Portland has been your home for decades now."

"And we're done with being here. I'm ready to move on. I think it's healthy to move on. I like the fact that Tyler will be closer to us in case we need him, as we age and need more help. So would you consider my proposal?"

Kate didn't want to talk because she felt like she would be blubbering like a baby. Her chest was wet already from the tears streaming down her cheeks. She inhaled and exhaled several times, trying to quell the torrential rain coming from her eyes.

"I'd be delighted, Mom. I think it would be a lot of fun. I'm not sure how much we have to spend, and that was bothering me because I couldn't see how we could have this, keep abreast financially, save for the kids' colleges, and all of that. So if you invest the money in the building and we have that built, then that solves that question. Perhaps in our partnership, we could put a portion of the proceeds to pay you back for your expenses."

"No, no, no, no, no. I want to make a donation to this partnership. The insurance money would be a donation from us and our future. To our family really. That money does not have to be repaid. Now if we decide to fix it up further or add on or expand it, then we can talk about sharing the costs there. But I'd like to have a gallery again, and you need a place to show what you can do with your catering and create income from setting up these destination weddings."

This was an unbelievable offer.

"Who knows where this will go? And I even think it would be fun to start that food truck. I rather think our Volkswagen van would be an excellent little food truck. Pull it right up to events, festivals. People would love it. It's beautifully restored. We can set it up so that we travel around to different places and show up at events, and it helps showcase some of your catering skills. I don't think you have to buy a big old school bus or a vegetable truck in order to do it. The van would be perfect. The other thing that's perfect about it is it's something I can drive. I'm not sure I can drive a big old truck. And I'd like to help."

"Mom, I had no idea you and I thought so much alike. But you blindsided me with all this. I never knew this was even in the works. I can't tell you how excited I am. Thank you for your offer."

She gulped in a deep breath.

"Your offer is gratefully accepted!"

CHAPTER 20

FOUR MONTHS LATER, Kate and Tyler had purchased a used Sprinter van and took off for Sonoma County for that visit with Nick and Devon and their kids. Kendall wouldn't stop jumping on the rear seats, which folded into a huge king bed they all could sleep in, with some squirming. Kate went back and strapped her into the seat and then made the boys do the same.

There was a TV in the rear, as well as near the front of the van, a full bathroom with a shower, and an efficiency kitchen with microwave and a huge refrigerator-freezer. In fact, this model was chosen because of the size of the refrigerator-freezer.

They were going to drive all day, taking turns, and would arrive later this evening.

They drove up, passing through all the different climate zones of California, some areas bucolic and green with farmland, others dusty and grey where they raised cattle. And, as they approached Sonoma County, the appearance of vineyards dotting the hills like corn rows started changing the scenery. Without wildfires, which had plagued them in years past, the sky was as blue as Tyler's eyes, just like the beautiful day when she first met him on the plane.

"You remember that plane ride, Tyler?"

"How could I forget?"

"Do you suppose any of our kids will meet someone that same way, like we did?"

"Hard to say. But if Kendall begins to read my sister's books, I think she has a good chance of becoming a hopeless romantic. And I wouldn't have it any other way."

She didn't want to ask about his plans, because they'd discussed it, and she promised she'd give him all the time he needed without trying to convince him one way or the other. It was so hard to do.

"I know what you want to ask me."

She was shocked. "Now I can add mind reader to your list of accomplishments?"

"Do you want to tease me with those lips of yours, your sparkly eyes, that sexy expression? And would you look what's happened to your skirt? Almost indecent, Mrs. Gray."

She glanced down at her lap and smiled. Had she done this on purpose?

"Do you want to hear?"

"I would. What do I have to do to earn it, though? I'd like to earn it."

"Oh my, Mrs. Gray. My pants are getting tight."

She glanced over her shoulder and saw their three kids glued to the dragon movie.

"Just wait until I get hold of you tonight. You best be very good and very careful," he said and showed his handsome smile that made her panties wet.

"So I have to wait, then?"

"Not at all. Kate, I'm in full agreement with the center, and you and Mom and Gretchen working on that. I think Linda wants to be a part of it too so she can sell some of her books, but don't give her anything to do with money, promise?"

She giggled. "I promise."

"I'm going to sign on to one more rotation. Then I'm going to ask Kyle for my papers. We're losing a lot of members, and recruitment is way down. I'm going to give Kyle a long window to get more members onto the team. He'll respect that decision. He may even be looking at doing the same, but that's his gig."

Kate wasn't disappointed, because he said he was willing to leave. Now she had to check on the rest of it.

"Are you doing this for me or for you? Is this decision something you'd make on your own?"

"One of the things I did and didn't tell you was

about going into the VA and having myself evaluated. I'm going to need a hip replacement, and sooner than we thought. My elbows are killing me most of the time, due to a fall. And my knees are getting close to bone on bone. Every day, they hurt just a little more. I don't want to be on pain meds my whole life. I want to be active. Having a hip replaced before you're forty is really bad. But in our line of work, it's very common. Knees too. So I want to separate, have the surgeries, and then spend a nice long recovery period with lots of physical therapy. I want to be healthy and active."

"I want that too. So you're doing it for you. I like that most of all."

IT WAS A balmy evening as they walked down the vineyards, heard the crickets chirping, felt the cool breeze in their faces, and could smell the faint hint of grapes growing on the vines. Baby grapes. Not the big black luscious ones or the tiny currant-type ones that would be coming up later. It was a nice, pleasant scent unlike any other kind of orchard, farm, or garden.

"I love it here too. And we do have choices," he said as he stopped and kissed the palm of her hand. "If you ever think you'd like to come back here, just say the word."

"Thank you. But anyplace you are is my home. Always, Tyler. I wouldn't mind visiting more often, and now with the van, maybe we can. It won't be as expensive with the kids this way. We can trade off with the driving duties. Bring our own food."

"Specially prepared gourmet food."

"That's right. Maybe you and I could work some festivals up here, too, expand our brand, like Devon and Nick do."

"I was thinking the same way."

"Your parents have the VW van. We have our Sprinter."

"And I like making love to you much better in the Sprinter," he said, drawing her into him.

"Yes, I like the leather seats and the room. It's perfect for us."

He kissed her then ran his finger down her lips. "So you're okay with this arrangement?"

"Which one are you talking about?" she asked. "The one where we come up here, do festivals, and you stay on the Teams for another rotation, or the one where you screw my brains out in the van tonight?"

"Both. I want it all, Kate. I want all of you, and I promise to give you all of me."

"Always, Tyler."

"Forever."

Did you like Heart of Gold, Tyler and Kate's second story? If you haven't read the book where they first met and fell in love, be sure to check out SEAL Of My Heart.

Or you can read all the SEAL Brotherhood books in The Ultimate SEAL Collection #1 and Ultimate SEAL Collection #2, then go to the entire series for SEAL Brotherhood: Legacy, which takes all the original couples in the SEAL Brotherhood and shows you what's happened ten years later after they marry, divorce, have families, and weather the storms of their jobs.

Other series you might like, featuring some of these same characters, as well as other SEALs:
Bad Boys of SEAL Team 3
Band of Bachelors
Bone Frog Brotherhood
Bone Frog Bachelor
Sunset SEALs

Almost all of these books are also out on audio book, narrated by the award-winning former Nashville Star and actor, J.D. Hart.

ABOUT THE AUTHOR

 NYT and USA/Today Bestselling Author Sharon Hamilton's SEAL Brotherhood series have earned her author rankings of #1 in Romantic Suspense, Military Romance and Contemporary Romance. Her other *Brotherhood* stand-alone series are: Bad Boys of SEAL Team 3, Band of Bachelors, True Blue SEALs, Nashville SEALs, Bone Frog Brotherhood, Sunset SEALs, Bone Frog Bachelor Series and SEAL Brotherhood Legacy Series. She is a contributing author to the very popular Shadow SEALs multi-author series.

Her SEALs and former SEALs have invested in two wineries, a lavender farm and a brewery in Sonoma County, which have become part of the new stories. They also have expanded to include Veteran-benefit projects on the Florida Gulf Coast, as well as projects in Africa and the Maldives. One of the SEAL wives has even launched her own women's fiction series. But old characters, as well as children of these SEAL heroes keep returning to all the newer books.

Sharon also writes sexy paranormals in two series: Golden Vampires of Tuscany and The Guardians under the pen name S. Hamil. She has a new Sci-Fi series, Free to Love, coming out in June of 2023 in a five book ultra-spicy series about an Android who falls in love with a human woman.

Annie Carr, Sharon's sweet romance author pen name, has just released her first book in 2023, I'll Always Love You, in Sunset Beach stories. She is planning this to become a multiple-book series.

A lifelong organic vegetable and flower gardener, Sharon and her husband lived for fifty years in the Wine Country of Northern California, where many of her stories take place. Recently, they have moved to the beautiful Gulf Coast of Florida, with stories of shipwrecks, the white sugar-sand beaches of Sunset, Treasure Island and Indian Rocks Beaches.

She loves hearing from fans through her website: authorsharonhamilton.com

Find out more about Sharon, her upcoming releases, appearances and news when you sign up for Sharon's newsletter.

Facebook:
facebook.com/SharonHamiltonAuthor

Twitter:
twitter.com/sharonlhamilton

Pinterest:

pinterest.com/AuthorSharonH

Amazon:

amazon.com/Sharon-Hamilton/e/B004FQQMAC

BookBub:

bookbub.com/authors/sharon-hamilton

Youtube:

youtube.com/channel/UCDInkxXFpXp_4Vnq08ZxM
BQ

Soundcloud:

soundcloud.com/sharon-hamilton-1

Sharon Hamilton's Rockin' Romance Readers:

facebook.com/groups/sealteamromance

Sharon Hamilton's Goodreads Group:

goodreads.com/group/show/199125-sharon-hamilton-
readers-group

Visit Sharon's Online Store:

sharon-hamilton-author.myshopify.com

Join Sharon's Review Teams:

eBook Reviews:

sharonhamiltonassistant@gmail.com

Audio Reviews:

sharonhamiltonassistant@gmail.com

Life is one fool thing after another.

Love is two fool things after each other.

REVIEWS

PRAISE FOR THE
GOLDEN VAMPIRES OF TUSCANY SERIES

"Well to say the least I was thoroughly surprise. I have read many Vampire books, from Ann Rice to Kym Grosso and few other Authors, so yes I do like Vampires, not the super scary ones from the old days, but the new ones are far more interesting far more human than one can remember. I found Honeymoon Bite a totally engrossing book, I was not able to put it down, page after page I found delight, love, understanding, well that is until the bad bad Vamp started being really bad. But seeing someone love another person so much that they would do anything to protect them, well that had me going, then well there was more and for a while I thought it was the end of a beautiful love story that spanned not only time but, spanned Italy and California. Won't divulge how it ended, but I did shed a few tears after screaming but Sharon Hamilton did not let me down, she took me on amazing trip that I loved, look forward to reading another Vampire book of hers."

"An excellent paranormal romance that was exciting, romantic, entertaining and very satisfying to read. It had me anticipating what would happen next many times over, so much so I could not put it down and even finished it up in a day. The vampires in this book were different from your average vampire, but I enjoy different variations and changes to the same old stuff. It made for a more unpredictable read and more adventurous to explore! Vampire lovers, any paranormal readers and even those who love the romance genre will enjoy Honeymoon Bite."

"This is the first non-Seal book of this author's I have read and I loved it. There is a cast-like hierarchy in this vampire community with humans at the very bottom and Golden vampires at the top. Lionel is a dark vampire who are servants of the Goldens. Phoebe is a Golden who has not decided if she will remain human or accept the turning to become a vampire. Either way she and Lionel can never be together since it is forbidden.

I enjoyed this story and I am looking forward to the next installment."

"A hauntingly romantic read. Old love lost and new love found. Family, heart, intrigue and vampires. Grabbed my attention and couldn't put down. Would definitely recommend."

PRAISE FOR THE
SEAL BROTHERHOOD SERIES

"Fans of Navy SEAL romance, I found a new author to feed your addiction. Finely written and loaded delicious with moments, Sharon Hamilton's storytelling satisfies like a thick bar of chocolate." —Marliss Melton, bestselling author of the *Team Twelve* Navy SEALs series

"Sharon Hamilton does an EXCELLENT job of fitting all the characters into a brotherhood of SEALS that may not be real but sure makes you feel that you have entered the circle and security of their world. The stories intertwine with each book before…and each book after and THAT is what makes Sharon Hamilton's SEAL Brotherhood Series so very interesting. You won't want to put down ANY of her books and they will keep you reading into the night when you should be sleeping. Start with this book…and you will not want to stop until you've read the whole series and then…you will be waiting for Sharon to write the next one." (5 Star Review)

"Kyle and Christy explode all over the pages in this first book, *[Accidental SEAL]*, in a whole new series of SEALs. If the twist and turns don't get your heart jumping, then maybe the suspense will. This is a must read for those that are looking for love and adventure with a little sloppy love thrown in for good measure." (5 Star Review)

PRAISE FOR THE
BAD BOYS OF SEAL TEAM 3 SERIES

"I love reading this series! Once you start these books, you can hardly put them down. The mix of romance and suspense keeps you turning the pages one right after another! Can't wait until the next book!" (5 Star Review)

"I love all of Sharon's Seal books, but [SEAL's Code] may just be her best to date. Danny and Luci's journey is filled with a wonderful insight into the Native American life. It is a love story that will fill you with warmth and contentment. You will enjoy Danny's journey to become a SEAL and his reasons for it. Good job Sharon!" (5 Star Review)

PRAISE FOR THE
BAND OF BACHELORS SERIES

"[Lucas] was the first book in the Band of Bachelors series and it was a phenomenal start. I loved how we got to see the other SEALs we all love and we got a look at Lucas and Marcy. They had an instant attraction, and their love was very intense. This book had it all, suspense, steamy romance, humor, everything you want in a riveting, outstanding read. I can't wait to read the next book in this series." (5 Star Review)

PRAISE FOR THE
TRUE BLUE SEALS SERIES

"Keep the tissues box nearby as you read *True Blue SEALs: Zak* by Sharon Hamilton. I imagine more than I wish to that the circumstances surrounding Zak and Amy are all too real for returning military personnel and their families. Ms. Hamilton has put us right in the middle of struggles and successes that these two high school sweethearts endure. I have read several of Sharon Hamilton's military romances but will say this is the most emotionally intense of the ones that I have read. This is a well-written, realistic story with authentic characters that will have you rooting for them and proud of those who serve to keep us safe. This is an author who writes amazing stories that you love and cry with the characters. Fans of Jessica Scott and Marliss Melton will want to add Sharon Hamilton to their list of realistic military romance writers." (5 Star Review)

"Dear FATHER IN HEAVEN,

If I may respectfully say so sometimes you are a strange God. Though you love all mankind,

It seems you have special predilections too.

You seem to love those men who can stand up alone who face impossible odds, Who challenge every bully and every tyrant ~

Those men who know the heat and loneliness of Calvary. Possibly you cherish men of this stamp because you recognize the mark of your only son in them.

Since this unique group of men known as the SEALs know Calvary and suffering, teach them now the mystery of the resurrection ~ that they are indestructible, that they will live forever because of their deep faith in you.

And when they do come to heaven, may I respectfully warn you, Dear Father, they also know how to celebrate. So please be ready for them when they insert under your pearly gates.

Bless them, their devoted Families and their Country on this glorious occasion.

We ask this through the merits of your Son, Christ Jesus the Lord, Amen."

By Reverend E.J. McMalhon S.J. LCDR, CHC, USN
Awards Ceremony SEAL Team One
1975 At NAB, Coronado